GIRLS' NIGHT OUT

HEART FALLS VIGNETTE COLLECTION: VOL. 2

VIVIAN AREND

Girls' Night Out
Copyright © 2022 by Arend Publishing Inc.
ISBN: 9781990674150
Edited by Angie Ramey
Cover Design © Damonza
Proofed by Manuela Velasco & Linda Levy

MESSAGE FROM VIVIAN

After the happily ever afters, *their* stories go on.

One of the great parts of writing a long family saga is revisiting characters who have already found their happily ever after. Once again, we're diving back into Heart Falls, only this time we're also sneaking a little ahead for a couple of stories.

This collection contains a ***brand-new*** short story for Walker and Ivy Stone as well. I'm so glad to be able to share this important moment in their lives.

Check the intros first to see where the individual stories fit into the full series if you want to avoid spoilers for books you haven't yet read! There's a reading order on the next page if you want to make sure you've read all the books so far. I will admit I overlap stories at times, though, so it's occasionally a bit of a tangle. Plus, I've jumped around a little between series, so if you've missed any, now's the time to catch up!

I've also included a who's who this go-round to help you remember names and places.

I hope these stories make you smile.

With love from me and your friends in Heart Falls.

HEART FALLS SERIES CHRONOLOGICAL READING ORDER

A Rancher's Heart (The Stones of Heart Falls, Book 1)

Surprised at Bootstomp Point (Heart Falls Vignette Collection Vol.1)

A Rancher's Song (The Stones of Heart Falls, Book 2)

A Firefighter's Christmas Gift (Holidays in Heart Falls, Book 1)

A Rancher's Bride (The Stones of Heart Falls, Book 3)

Heartfelt at Heart Falls (Heart Falls Vignette Collection Vol.1)

The Cowgirl's Forever Love (The Colemans of Heart Falls, Book 1)

A Wild Horse Wedding (Heart Falls Vignette Collection Vol.1)

The Cowgirl's Secret Love (The Colemans of Heart Falls, Book 2)

The Cowgirl's Chosen Love (The Colemans of Heart Falls, Book 3)

Glamour & Truth (Heart Falls Vignette & Novella Collection: Vol. 2)

A Soldier's Christmas Wish (Holidays in Heart Falls, Book 2)

Oh, Baby! (Heart Falls Vignette Collection Vol.1)

A Hero's Christmas Hope (Holidays in Heart Falls, Book 3)

Ashton's Birthday Surprise (Heart Falls Vignette & Novella Collection: Vol. 2)

A Rancher's Love (The Stones of Heart Falls, Book 4)

A Cowboy's Christmas List (Holiday in Heart Falls, Book 4)

Mischief at the Fire Hall (Heart Falls Vignette & Novella Collection: Vol. 2)

A Rancher's Christmas Kiss (Holiday in Heart Falls, Book 5)

Sharing Secrets (Heart Falls Vignette & Novella Collection: Vol. 2)

A Forever Family (Heart Falls Vignette & Novella Collection: Vol. 2)

Rose's One Night to Forever (Heart Falls Vignette & Novella Collection: Vol. 3)

Still to come:

A Cowboy's Claim (The Skyes of Heart Falls, Book 1)

A Cowboy's Bride (The Skyes of Heart Falls, Book 2)

A Cowboy's Trust (The Skyes of Heart Falls, Book 3)

And others.

Heart Falls

during **Girls' Night Out** *Vignette Collection*

Book 14 in series

Whiskey Creek
Colemans
george & sally (d)

Karen & Finn Marlette
6. The Cowgirl's Secret Love

The Stone
Family
walter(d) & deb(d)

Caleb & Tamara

sasha, emma, tyler
1. A Rancher's Heart

The Fields
Family
malachi & sophie

Luke & Kelli
4. A Rancher's Bride

Lisa & Josiah Ryder
Zoe, expecting
5. The Cowgirl's Forever Love
9. Oh Baby (Vignettes Vol 1)

Ivy & Walker

adopting
2. A Rancher's Song
14. A Forever Family (Vignettes Vol 2)

Julia & Zach Sorenson ***
7. The Cowgirl's Chosen Love

Rose & ???
15. Rose's One Night to Forever

Ginny & Tucker Stewart
11. A Rancher's Love

Heart Falls Firehall

Brad Ford and Hanna Lane
Chrissy, Drew
3. A Firefighter's Christmas Gift

Tansy

Dustin
??. A Rancher's Vow

Mack Klassen & Brooke Silver
expecting
8. A Soldier's Christmas Wish

Fern
??. Fern's Date with Destiny

Ryan Zhao & Madison Joy
Talia, expecting
10. A Hero's Christmas Hope

Alex Thorne & Yvette Wright
12. A Cowboy's Christmas List

Ashton Stewart** & Sonora Fallen*
13. A Rancher's Christmas Kiss

** Matriach of the Fields family*
*** Uncle to Tucker and foreman at Silver Stone ranch*
**** Married twice. It's complicated--go read The Cowgirl's Chosen Love*

GLAMOUR & TRUTH

Girls' night out is always a special evening. This time, Julia Blushing will not only enjoy the company but learn a few lessons about making her guy happy. And when we jump to just before the new year, Zach Sorenson gets a special reminder of exactly how well she learned that lesson!

Featuring: Hanna Ford, Tamara Stone, Karen Marlette, Lisa Coleman, and Julia Blushing. (AKA, the four Whiskey Creek sisters and Hanna from *A Firefighter's Christmas Gift*.)

Timeline: This scene starts during **The Cowgirl's Chosen Love**

1

JULIA

November, Lone Pine ranch

"I've got all the extra bits and pieces we need." Hanna Ford gestured at the fabric piled on her living room table. "Only this part isn't my forte. I'm a cleanup kind of girl. Making the mess is a little harder."

Julia Blushing laughed as she stepped forward to help her new friend. Since arriving in Heart Falls the previous April, she'd had plenty of time to get to know her sisters and some of the women in the community.

Tonight's girls' night out activity promised to be an eye-opener, in more ways than one.

A week earlier Hanna had looped Julia in and suggested that they set up a boudoir shoot. They'd brainstormed how to run the session in a low-key way, acting as their own photographers. When they emailed the idea to everyone in their group, along with a list of items to bring, the plan was greeted with enthusiasm. A few members of their regular group couldn't make it, but the ones who could were fully on board.

Hanna's husband, Brad, hadn't been told the details, but he'd willingly taken their daughter out for the evening to leave the house empty for mischief.

"I can take care of this part," Julia promised. "You finish getting the rest of the important stuff together."

"You mean the food and drinks? That I have under control," Hanna said.

"Pour me a drink, then, because I think we'll all need something under our belts before we start." Julia picked up one of the sheets Hanna had left on the table and began strategically draping it over a couple of chairs and pinning it to the curtains as a backdrop.

She'd barely finished when Hanna held forward a tumbler full of ice and something fruity. "Here. Strawberry mojito. Not very festive, but also not tequila."

"Thanks." Julia laughed before she tucked the final edge of the sheet between two chair cushions then took the liquid offering. She lifted it in a toast. "To an evening full of *lots* of blushing."

Hanna's cheeks flushed. "So it would seem. But since this is self-inflicted, I've got nobody to blame but me."

Before Julia could respond, a loud bang and shout rang from the front door. "Hello. We're letting ourselves in."

A moment later Julia's three sisters entered the room together, conversation swelling as if there were a dozen of them. Tamara caught Hanna in a hug, Karen put down an armload of snacks, and Lisa went straight to the draped fabric, hands planted on her hips as she examined it decisively.

"Make yourself at home," Hanna said without a trace of sarcasm. The petite woman was just so damn sweet and innocent, which made it all the funnier that she was the one who'd come up with the theme for the evening.

Lisa twirled, rubbing her hands together. "I cannot believe it took this long for us to have a boudoir shoot. I am so looking forward to this."

"It'll be fun," Tamara agreed, "but let's make a pact right now. All pictures stay private unless *we* choose to put them out there."

"Definitely." Hanna nodded seriously. "Part of the reason I didn't hire a real photographer was the money, but also, even if none of the pictures we take on our phones turn out great, we'll still have the fun of doing something together."

Karen had found the pitcher of drinks and poured a round for everyone. "Trust me, odds are we'll have at least a few good pictures in the end."

"Screw the pictures," Lisa said with exaggerated flair. "I mean, I agree in principle. Considering how awesome the material, the pictures are bound to turn out gorgeous." She gestured to the women around her. "But the whole point of boudoir is to celebrate our amazingness and absolute personification of sexiness."

"In other words, a *fuck you* to a society that says my post-baby body is no longer drool-worthy?" Tamara asked with a smile. She'd settled on the couch, the rest of the group gathering around and getting comfortable.

"Pretty much," Hanna agreed.

"I will say I have a fairly healthy attitude toward my body, and yes, I'm looking forward to celebrating that. But I'm also looking for a good Christmas present for Finn. Because not only are these pictures going to make me happy, but I really hope one or two make him happy as well," Karen said.

Tamara raised her glass. "Hallelujah, Hanna. You solved my Christmas dilemma. Our husbands will *all* say thank you down the road."

"Oops, we'd better kick Lisa out," Karen teased. "No husband."

Julia held her tongue. She and Zach were legally married, but their actual relationship was a lot more complicated.

"Shut up. Just because you decided you wanted to put a ring on it, doesn't mean Josiah and I have to cave to antiquated societal norms. Permanently shacking up is like a step beyond marriage because there's no paperwork demanding we stick together." Lisa dipped her chin firmly then stuck out her tongue. "So there."

A trickle of laughter danced around the room. "For a moment I was going to say that was an amazingly mature thought process, but then you had to go and reveal your true colours at the end." Tamara clucked disapprovingly, dodging the pillow Lisa tossed at her.

"Speaking of sex," Lisa began.

Karen snorted, wiping at her mouth as she apologized. "*Were* we speaking of sex?"

"We were bound to at some point," Lisa said pragmatically. She leaned forward. "Just an FYI, since lifelong learning is a goal I aspire to, I found this wildly entertaining website last week. WowYes."

Julia and the others paused as Lisa fell silent.

"We're waiting. Great podcasts? YouTube? Cooking show? Oh, wait. You said sex." Julia pretended to be shocked. "You're sending us to a porn site?"

"Oh, I wouldn't dream of ruining your fun. Just thought I'd share that I bought a membership. Josiah and I are working through some of the suggestions, and totally TMI, but holy fucking moly, I might have passed out from my orgasm the other night."

Hanna's cheeks were glowing hot enough to heat the entire room. "Um. Good for you?"

Tamara patted Hanna on the arm. "It takes all types, honey, and Lisa's definitely an *extra* type. Exhibitionist, extrovert, extra out-there."

"Hey, I resemble that remark." Lisa winked at her own bad joke.

Tamara put her glass down decisively. "Okay, somebody's gotta go first, so to get this show onto a slightly less risqué topic, I volunteer. Let me get changed."

She stood, grabbing an oversize purse off the table and heading to the bathroom.

"Any ideas where you want to pose?" Hanna tossed after her.

Tamara glanced back over her shoulder, a mischievous smile flashing. "Let's use the kitchen."

She vanished from sight, leaving Julia to exchange confused but happy smiles with the three remaining women.

"Well, this could be interesting." Julia got to her feet, bringing out her phone. "Hanna, did you find any suggestions for the best way to take shots?"

"A few. Don't use terrible props. Watch the angle of your shots so it doesn't feel as if the model is about to tip over. Don't take pictures from too far away, don't try to get too close. Try not to chop off limbs—"

"Always a good suggestion when you're taking pictures in a kitchen," Lisa quipped. She moved aside one of the chairs at the kitchen table, glancing around the neat area with an assessing eye. "I guess we'll wait to see what Tamara has in mind."

It didn't take long before Coleman sister number two returned, her dark hair combed straight over her shoulders, a fuzzy robe wrapped around her long, sturdy body. "I'm ready for my debut," Tamara teased.

She walked to the sink and pivoted, resting her hands on the counter behind her hips.

Lisa had her phone out, but she sniffed disapprovingly. "Hon, hate to tell you this, but the instructions said to bring something to wear that made you feel, you know, *glamorous.*

This is what you look like every morning. I know this because I lived with you for six months."

"Scratch that. We lived with her for *years*, and this is what she's always looked like in the morning," Karen corrected.

"Except for that time when she had the hair disaster." Lisa shook her head, a horrified expression crossing her face.

"Dear Lord, that's right." A shudder shook Karen's torso.

"The bangs. The bangs were simply—"

"Oh my God, shut *up*," Tamara said with a laugh, pushing her crimson glasses a little more firmly on her nose. She turned her gaze to Hanna and Julia. "I'd apologize for those two, but they're not my responsibility."

Hanna giggled. "You guys are terrible to each other, but it's clear how much you love being terrible to each other. I like that."

Tamara winked then clapped her hands decisively. "All right. Enough teasing. This is me, celebrating my awesomeness, six months post-baby, a bunch of years post-eighteen." She turned her gaze on Lisa. "And I'll have you know, part of what makes me feel powerful and complete is that I have an amazing husband and incredible children. They aren't *who* I am, but they've filled a part in me that makes me happy. And the robe in the morning is a part of that."

"Preach it, sister," Lisa offered enthusiastically. "Fuzzy robe your heart out, then."

Tamara brought out her own phone, cranking up a country station. She put it on the counter a few paces away before facing the gathering. "Here we go. You tell me if I need to change position, since I can't see what you're looking at."

She let the robe fall open as she leaned back on the counter. Her gaze rested somewhere near the door to the kitchen. It looked as if she'd made eye contact with a certain someone—in her case, Caleb—whom she was about to get naughty with.

Under the robe she wore a push-up bra and boy shorts, the

same crimson as her glasses. The contrast between the robe and the lingerie underneath showed two sides of a coin. A get-it-done mom and a woman who definitely knew she was attractive to the man in her world.

What followed was laughter and whistles of admiration and cheeks that didn't need any makeup to turn them rosy and bright. Julia helped take pictures, making suggestions as to where Tamara should stand and how to adjust her poses.

"Oh, look at this one." Hanna stepped forward and showed Tamara her screen.

"Damn. That is hot. *I'm* hot," Tamara said with a grin before offering Hanna a high five. "Hang on, I want to take a few more without the robe, but I think we've got some good ones. These are going to make Caleb very happy."

Ten minutes later, Tamara was back in her jeans and T-shirt, flipping through the pictures on Karen's phone as they waited for Lisa to join them.

"Oh, my." Hanna's whispered words hung on the air.

Three heads turned to discover Lisa strutting into the living room as if she were on a fashion runway. "You like?"

"How the hell are you not breaking your ankles?" Tamara demanded, pointing down at what had to be four-inch heels in shiny black gracing Lisa's feet.

Julia had an even more pressing question. "How the hell are you not falling out of those scraps of material?"

Lisa shimmied her shoulders, and the straps of black crossing her bosom in an imitation of a bra flowed with her as if they were drawn on. "Two-sided tape," she confessed.

She pivoted, showing off the short black skirt and fishnet stockings. Then she brandished the final part of her costume—a feather duster.

"You're sexy *and* making me laugh," Karen offered. "I had no idea you had French maid fantasies. Is this why you wanted to travel?"

"Hush," Lisa said in a very dignified voice. Then she winked. "I'm with Tamara. I do think a boudoir shoot is an amazing way to celebrate our confidence, but it's also a really good opportunity to do something nice for my guy. And at the risk of being TMI again, this outfit is going to make Josiah very happy. I like doing things that make him smile, in all parts of our relationship."

Warmth rushed through Julia. The evening had begun with her thinking how wonderful it was to celebrate her sisters and positive womanhood, but truthfully—Zach was on her mind.

The whole situation between them had been a roller coaster for the past two and a half months. They still had a long time to go before they fulfilled the terms that bound them, but spending time with him wasn't a chore.

Hearing Lisa and Tamara so casually talking about things that made their guys happy made her think about Zach. The things he'd done to help her deal with her changing world. To help face her challenges.

What would make him happy?

Julia pushed her thoughts aside for a moment and got back into the evening. Taking pictures of Lisa, and then Karen, who didn't even leave the room to get ready for her shoot.

The oldest of the Coleman girls did make them head into the nearby barn, though. "We need the right ambience in the background." Karen undid the top buttons on her flannel shirt and leaned back on the rough wood of a horse's stall.

A sky-blue camisole peeked into view. The longer they took pictures, the more buttons Karen slowly opened as her lips lifted in a secretive smile.

When she undid the buttons of her jeans and slipped the flannel off completely, Hanna waved a hand in front of her face. "Wow. You guys are dangerous. And hot. I mean, it's hot in here, right?"

Laughter bounced around them.

"Why, thank you." Karen winked. "Okay, Hanna. You ready to show us what you've got?"

Hanna pressed her hands to her cheeks then nodded decisively. "If you don't mind, I'd like to take pictures in my bedroom."

Four sisters exchanged glances but moved with amazing restraint, the teasing temporarily eased. It was clear Hanna had an agenda and was determined to follow through no matter how embarrassed she was.

When she came out of the bathroom, she wore a man's white dress shirt, obviously one of Brad's, and not much else.

"Hanna." Tamara spoke softly from where they were gathered by the door of the bedroom. "You are very beautiful."

Hanna's eyes sparkled, her dark hair draped over one shoulder, cheeks a brilliant red. "Thank you. Now, before I lose my nerve, we should start."

She crawled on the bed then sat demurely for the first while. Legs together, hands curled around her knees. It took a bit, but slowly Hanna relaxed. Undoing a few buttons, hugging a pillow in front of her before stretching out and smiling as if Brad were right there.

"You look amazing," Julia assured her, and they continued to chat easily during the next busy moments. Finally she offered Hanna a nod. "I got a couple of great shots."

"Me too. Anything else you want, hon?" Tamara asked.

Hanna twisted to her knees. She hesitated, the cool confidence she'd gathered vanishing behind her blush. "I want somebody to take a picture—I can't believe I'm saying this—from lying on the bed."

"You want one of us to lie down?" Karen asked.

Hanna squeezed her eyes tight as she nodded. She took a shaky breath then whispered in a rush, "Brad likes it when I'm on top. I want to give him a picture like that."

It was a moment of such pure honesty and a confession so

filled with love, there was no embarrassment at hearing the shared intimacy.

Lisa had already moved, sliding onto her back with her phone at the ready. "Brad is a very lucky man."

Hanna took a deep breath, her embarrassment fading as pure, honest adoration slid in. "He's my heart. He's my everything."

The room fell silent as Lisa clicked pictures.

"Okay, I got it. No, wait, just one more thing." Lisa reached beside her and grabbed a pillow before curling upright and swinging the fluffy weapon at Hanna with a burst of laughter. "Pillow fight."

The bit of tension that had slipped into the room vanished, and while pillows swung and laughter rose, Hanna stole away to get dressed.

When she rejoined them in the living room, she offered everyone an enormous hug before lifting her chin. "We're all going to just forget that happened, aren't we?"

Karen shook her head. "We will never speak of it again, but I am never forgetting. Hanna, sweetheart, you were willing to make yourself vulnerable in order to give Brad something that will make him really happy. You just showed me an example of love I'm going to try to live up to when it comes to Finn."

Hanna nodded briskly, fighting back tears. "Okay. But we're done discussing it, right? It's Julia's turn."

So many things rushed through Julia's mind.

"It'll only take me a minute to get ready," she promised. Like Karen, she'd come prepared, already wearing her simple outfit.

Only as she took off her sweater to reveal the white tank top underneath, her focus wasn't on the pictures they were about to take.

She wanted the picture for herself. What did *Zach* want? *Truly* want?

Julia had a pretty good idea of one thing that would make

him happy. It was something he would never suspect was coming, and yet...

She was ready to try.

The first part of the evening finished, and they ended up in the living room, scrolling through pictures on their phones and sharing the best ones. Laughter and companionship and a deep sense of being connected had turned it into an extraordinary evening.

But the question in Julia's brain remained. Was she ready to give Zach something that would make him truly happy?

2

———

ZACH

A month and a half later. December 31, Red Boot ranch.

Zach woke, momentarily disoriented. He pushed upright in the bed, hand sliding over the dip in the sheets next to him.

The spot where Julia usually lay was still warm. And considering the sheets were pushed back and not neatly pulled into place, which was not at all like her, he hoped whatever had taken her out of their cozy retreat was a temporary thing.

"Jules?"

With no deadlines beyond a family gathering that evening, there was no reason they couldn't laze about the entire morning. In fact, Julia had promised something to that effect when they'd gotten back from Hawaii late the night before, which was why her being gone was doubly disappointing.

The door cracked open.

"You're supposed to still be asleep," she complained before shouldering her way into the room, coffee cups in her hands.

Zach adjusted position, reaching to help her. "I want to enjoy whatever mischief you've got planned for this morning."

"Then this should wake you up," she said with a smile. "Good morning."

He took a couple deep swallows of his coffee then sighed with contentment. "Damn, that's good."

Julia leaned up against the pillows before adjusting the sheets over her lap, turning the edge of the quilt perfectly straight. Then she grabbed her own cup and drank as well.

Zach eyed her. Something was up. "What did you do?"

Her eyes widened over the top of her cup. She lowered it, all innocent and demure. "Me? Whatever are you talking about?"

Oh, no. Not only had he spent the past four months getting to know Julia very intimately, but that tingling in his gut was back. He carefully put his cup aside before reaching for the one in her fingers and stealing it in spite of her protest.

"Hey, I'm not done with that."

He placed it beside his on the side table then rolled toward her. Kneeling over her with their faces level. "*Julia.*"

She snorted, hand brushing up to cover her mouth.

He was going to have to pull out the big guns to get her to fess up. So be it. Zach stripped back the bedsheets, caught hold of her hips, and shoved her a foot lower on the bed. She laughed as the pillows bounced away, and he ended up trapping her body under his.

"So much for a relaxing morning in bed with my coffee and a book," Julia complained.

"Tell me what secrets you're keeping." He teased his lips against the side of her neck and nibbled on her earlobe until she quivered.

"*Zach.*" Her voice had gone husky, her breathing erratic. "I have a present for you."

He hummed happily, pushing aside the tank top she wore

to reveal one sweet breast. "I love it. It's exactly what I wanted," he said an instant before pressing a kiss against her skin.

Julia's legs wrapped around him, her fingers stroking through his hair. "You're terrible. But don't stop. You can have your real present later."

Zach wasn't so sure about that. She was in his bed, sighing sweetly and gasping at all the right moments, letting him touch her, and love her, and please her—

There was no present more real than this.

Still, when they finally made it out of bed and regrouped at the kitchen table, Julia took a wrapped present and placed it in front of him.

He eyed it with confusion. "It's no longer Christmas or my birthday. And considering I got exactly what I wanted for my birthday—you—what's this?"

Her nose wrinkled. "Remember the last girls' night out I went to?"

Hell yeah. "I'm never going to forget."

He winked. That night had put sex on the table for them and led to so much more.

Julia motioned to the wrapped present. "I didn't feel right bringing that to your parents' place in Hawaii. I felt awkward giving it to you anyway, but now that we're an *us*, I want you to have it."

With no further delay, Zach unwrapped a picture frame with a photo that made his mouth go dry and his heart leap.

It caused reactions in other parts of his body as well.

"Holy shit, this is gorgeous." He glanced up. "You are so fucking sexy."

Her lashes fluttered for a moment, not in pretense, but as if she was really pleased with his response. "I liked how it turned out, and I wanted to share it with you."

In the photo, she had her fingers tucked into her front pockets, ankles crossed, while leaning against a solid wood door that looked as if it'd been around since the turn of the century. Faded blue jeans caressed her legs, the same faded-to-sinfully-soft pair he'd drooled over back before they'd even gotten together.

A white tank top clung to her curves, her hair draped over her shoulders. She stared straight into the camera as if challenging the world. The attitude was sexy as fuck, no doubt about it.

"Am I admitting I'm an animal if I tell you I can see your nipples and I'm currently hard as a rock?" Zach glanced across the table.

Julia's lips curled upward. "I slipped off my bra, and it was a little cold in the room. Very unplanned and yet, yes, I agree. I feel like a goddess when I look at that picture."

Zach was out of his chair, picture placed carefully on the table.

"You are a goddess. *My* goddess." He scooped Julia up in his arms and kissed her, worshiping her lips the way that he wanted to worship all of her, with all of him, for all the years to come.

They finally broke apart. Julia was wrapped around him, smiling contentedly. "Happy New Year, baby."

It was going to be. They had nine months to wait until their wedding, and there would be challenges and more things to learn. But as long as they did it together, with friends and family at their side, it would all work out.

He leaned their foreheads together and looked her in the eye. "Happy New Year, love."

~

IF YOU'VE NEVER READ about what happened *after* this girls' night out, pick up **THE COWGIRL'S CHOSEN LOVE** .

ASHTON'S BIRTHDAY SURPRISE

Ashton Stewart is enjoying having his nephew around Silver Stone ranch full-time. Maybe now Ashton will be able to put more energy into solving the riddle of how to deal with that woman. The impossible one who drives him around the bend with such ease. Sonora Fallen.

Only not even an evening celebrating his birthday with friends can wipe her from his thoughts. Especially since Sonora has some plans of her own.

Featuring: Ashton Stewart, Tucker Stewart, Luke Stone, Josiah Ryder, Gary Silver (mechanic and dad from *A Soldier's Christmas Wish*), and others. Also Sonora Fallen.

Timeline: This story is set in January during **A Rancher's Love.**

1

ASHTON

January 15, Heart Falls

shton Stewart glared at his best friend. "What aren't you telling me?"

The stiff truck seat jostled them roughly as Gary hit a rut, the snow not deep enough to smooth the rough gravel surface. He kept his gaze forward, but his expression slipped into amusement. "No idea what you're talking about."

"Liar."

Gary Silver pressed one hand to his chest even as he kept a firm grip on the wheel with the other. "You wound me."

"I will if I have to," Ashton growled.

His friend snorted. "You could try."

Jeez. They sounded as bad as Ashton's nephew bickering with the Stone boys. Although those boys were now in their thirties and forties. Damn time passing.

Which was exactly what they were supposed to be celebrating today. Time passing. As in, Ashton's birthday. That should have meant he got to call the shots, but with his friends, there were no guarantees.

When Gary failed to turn at the proper spot to head to Rough Cut for their expected pool game and beers, Ashton simply sighed and leaned back, folding his arms over his chest. "What're you up to?" he mumbled. "It *is* my birthday. I think I deserve at least a warning."

"Because you don't think so well on your feet anymore?" Gary teased. "Good thing you brought Tucker on to help deal with your job. You're so long in the tooth, you're going to be put out to pasture with those retiree horses of yours."

"Why are we friends?" Ashton asked grumpily.

"Because you like it when people give you hell, and you are truly disappointed it doesn't happen more often." Gary's low chuckle didn't break when Ashton bounced a fist off his shoulder.

By now, they were past all the turnoffs into Heart Falls proper, which probably meant a longer drive to one of the neighbouring towns. "I hope you remember you promised me a birthday dinner," Ashton prodded his friend. "Preferably sometime in the next hour."

"Trust me."

When Gary didn't elaborate, Ashton shook his head and resisted the urge to complain the way one of the children from Silver Stone would've.

Instead, he eased back in the comfortable truck seat. "I like your new ride," he told Gary. "I might have to look at doing an upgrade myself."

That familiar rumble of amusement drifted from his friend again. "Yeah, the heated seats are a pretty nice touch for our ancient bodies."

Trust Gary to cut straight to the point.

Ashton nodded. "Damn right. If we've got to deal with

Alberta winters, we may as well have something to take the ache off the old bones."

You're the one who thinks you're old.

The words—said in a sassy, nerve-rattling, brain-tangling feminine lilt—drifted through Ashton's brain far too easily.

The source of the taunt? Sonora Fallen. Ashton's number one...

Annoyance? Temptation?

Was there really any way to define what they were to each other without a master chart and an empty afternoon?

Not for the first time, Ashton was grateful for the companionable silence between him and his best friend. It made it easy to stare out the window at the passing snowfields and let his tangled thoughts drift, because this was the one topic he avoided discussing with anyone.

Sonora could just as effortlessly bring a smile to his face as a reaction to his body or a flare to his temper.

To say they had a difficult relationship would be putting it mildly.

Thank God tonight was all about a retreat with his guys. A man needed that, especially when the womanly company around him wasn't peaceful and smooth. While someday Ashton planned to figure out how to make him and Sonora work without their tempers constantly boiling over, today was not that day.

Gary slowed the truck, making a careful turn onto an unexpected driveway.

Ashton leaned forward, glancing up the well-traveled road. "You need something from Josiah Ryder's?"

"Yep."

Ashton thought for a moment then sighed heavily again. "Damn those boys. This is what they've been whispering about in the corners of the barn for the past week."

Gary lifted his shoulders easily. "Don't know about that, but we've reached our destination for the night." He glanced at Ashton briefly before turning back to focus on the road to the local veterinarian's homestead. "Don't worry. I made them promise to not do anything that involved candles on a cake, or strippers, or shit like that."

As if. Ashton snickered. "Yeah. I'd get a kick out of seeing you explain strippers in her house to Lisa Ryder."

"Oh, she was more worried about the sixty-five candles setting off her fire alarms," Gary teased.

Ashton lifted a hand and flashed his friend the bird. "You'd think that the birthday boy would get some respect."

"Don't know why I should start that now."

"Ass." But Ashton said it with affection.

As unexpected as the birthday celebration twist was, walking in the door to discover the entire living room was full of men from the community, both from his generation and his nephew's, felt very satisfying.

His nephew was there talking to the vet, and both Tucker and Josiah stepped forward to greet him.

"Happy birthday, Uncle Ashton."

"Happy birthday, Ashton," Josiah echoed then gestured with a hand past the living room to the kitchen, where a table was piled high. "I made them promise to not sing, so let's start with some food—"

"And a drink," Tucker added helpfully.

Josiah dipped his chin. "Definitely a drink. Time to get this party started."

The next hour was pretty much what Ashton would've asked for if he could've come right out and named the best possible way to celebrate. The food was basic but tasty, with burgers and pizza and a massive amount of high-calorie finger foods. All of it totally worth it, despite the fact he'd have to up his exercising for the next few days to stay on an even keel.

He nursed a second drink, though. Chicken wings, he could

burn off. He wasn't sure what these hooligans would do to him if he tied one on too hard.

Everyone flowed through the room, changing seats to chat with new people on a regular basis. Ashton kept his amusement to himself when he realized he was being kept in one spot while everyone else did the shifting and regular deliveries of more snacks showed up at his elbow.

One of his regular pool-night buddies sat in the easy chair kitty-corner to him, the footrest raised and a beer in his hand. James sighed happily. "Damn nice of you to have a birthday in January. It was a great reason to get out."

Ashton grinned. "I did it just for you, James."

James waved a hand. "Of course you did." He suddenly leaned forward, something a lot more diabolical in his expression. "I think we should partner up for the rest of the evening's entertainment."

Okay...

Ashton eyed his friend. "What are you not telling me?"

James grinned. "You don't expect us to stop the celebrating after just a burger and a beer, do you?"

Shit. Now came the part of the evening where Ashton wasn't sure he'd be able to control the energy. He glanced around the room at the twenty-plus men and calculated the odds of the evening going sideways. "Anything I need to put the RCMP on speed dial for?"

A loud burst of laughter escaped James. "Trust us," he said earnestly.

Ashton eyed him sardonically. "Really? You said that with a straight face?"

Before James could respond, Tucker strode forward. He clapped his hands to get everyone's attention. "If you're all sufficiently stuffed, grab yourself a drink reload, and we'll get to the official challenge of the evening."

Challenge?

Ashton leaned back in his chair and folded his arms over his chest. "You're not thinking of playing kids' games like pin the tail on the donkey, are you?"

A loud hoot went up from the gathered men. "Told you we couldn't put one past him," Luke Stone said, wiggling a finger at Ashton's nephew.

Well, damn. Ashton had been joking.

He rose and met Tucker, who was waiting to direct him farther into the house. "I hope you know what you're doing," Ashton warned Tucker.

"Celebrating your birthday in a way that will never be forgotten," Tucker told him jovially.

At the top of the stairs, Ashton took two steps into the room then paused, trying to take it all in. He'd been in the open space before, years ago, but tonight, with the sun already below the horizon, it wasn't the fantastic view outside the second-storey windows that caught his attention.

Nope, it was the half dozen card tables set up all around the room, chairs at each one. In the center of each table sat one of Josiah's vintage children's games.

"Come on, friend. Let's see what I can beat you at first." Gary pointed to a nearby table that had a vertical tic-tac-toe board on it.

Pandemonium followed.

Laughter and loud roars became the rule of the evening. One table held the classic Rock 'Em Sock 'Em Robots, and the men playing with the Blue Bomber and Red Rocker might have been wagering a world boxing championship based on the cheers rising from the table.

The only thing louder were the shouts from the table where the Battling Tops war raged. Luke's top bounced out of bounds of the arena and landed in Tucker's beer, and they both shouted, for different reasons.

Josiah had even put out Jenga and Kerplunk, which required steadier hands than men who'd tipped back a few.

An hour later, Ashton's face was sore from grinning so much. It was ridiculous how much fun he was having playing silly childish games, especially after the first few minutes had proven there wasn't a man in the room who felt the need to pump out any macho crap.

Oh, some pretty intense competition was going on, but nothing involving swaggering, angry cursing, or outright fighting.

Not that these men were incapable of throwing a few punches, but after spending his days making sure it didn't happen on the ranch, it was nice to have a break.

He and Tucker partnered up against Luke and Caleb Stone on the Foosball table in what could only be considered a death match. Hands on the rods, they spun and kicked and shouted and behaved like kids hyped up on too much sugar.

All things considered, Ashton thought it was a damn good birthday celebration.

Later in the evening, he took a break from the active games. Didn't mean he got treated with kid gloves, though. Ashton shook his head as his best friend offered the killing stroke.

"Ha, B8, and that's the win for me." Gary shot his fists in the air and roared. "Say it. Say it loud."

"You sunk my battleship." Ashton rose to his feet, slapping Gary on the shoulder as he stepped toward the stairs. "Hold down the fort. I need some air."

"Will do." Gary eyed the room then waved over one of the younger men as they eagerly reset the playing boards. "Prepare to be humiliated."

Ashton chuckled the entire way downstairs.

A moment of quiet was good after the excitement and ruckus of the party. He paused to grab a drink of water from the kitchen, staring out the window, a foolish grin still stretching his face. He had good friends. Good people around him, and in spite of the things he didn't have, he was happy to celebrate sixty-five years on this earth.

Out in Josiah's backyard, a ghostly figure moved from behind a tree. A slight figure, wrapped in fabric that fluttered in the wintry wind.

Ashton frowned, stepping quickly toward the kitchen door that led onto the deck. What on earth was Lisa Ryder doing out in the cold dressed like that?

As he reached the edge of the deck, the figure scurried up the ramp that led to the children's tree house, the faintest glow of what looked like candlelight shining from the windows.

The hell? Ashton glanced down at his slippers and decided they would do for now. He walked carefully over the crusted snow to the nearest staircase, making his way into the yard. The snow crouched lightly underfoot as he stepped toward the tree house, the freezing January temperatures wrapping around him like icy fingers.

His phone buzzed with a message, and he paused for just long enough to pull it out and glance at the screen.

Sonora.

2

SONORA

Sonora knew exactly what she wanted to give Ashton for his birthday. They were both old enough and well-enough established that *things* weren't always the right answer.

Considering they were on again, off again with their relationship—ha! Even calling it a relationship was pushing the limits.

No. They definitely had a relationship, yet even after all these years, giving it a title was still impossible. A friendship of some sort. Secret lovers, to be sure. *Persistent annoyance* was also accurate.

But in spite of having *what* they were up in the air, milestones still deserved to be celebrated. Sonora had made that a lifetime rule, and she wasn't going to mess with it now.

Tucker's elaborate plans to hijack his uncle's birthday party for a guys' night out was brilliant. So what if it made giving Ashton her gift a little harder?

She was never one to back down from a challenge.

It had taken three trips to bring everything she needed out to the tree house, and that was only because she'd sweet-talked

Lisa into setting up the key component earlier in the day, which would've been logistically impossible to manage on her own.

That had meant bringing Lisa into her confidence, but the young woman already seemed to know everything going on in the community anyway—one way or another.

Lisa also knew how to keep her mouth shut, a skill Sonora appreciated. Especially while she and Ashton carried on their seemingly unending dance.

Someday they'd figure it out. Hopefully.

They damn well better.

Sonora set a match to the candle beside her then reached for her phone. Getting Ashton alone for a period of time was the only part of the evening she wasn't sure about.

It was all good and well to set up a surprise for the man, but knowing him, he could just as easily have left his phone at home or have a dead battery. Ashton and technology were so annoying.

Yet she simply couldn't get enough of him.

She took a deep breath, pushed away her frustrations, and hoped for the best.

SONORA: *Happy birthday. Having fun?*

SHE STARED AT THE PHONE, waiting to see if she got any kind of response.

Wood creaked outside. She snapped her head up as the door of the tree house swung open, and there he was. Ashton, a crease between his brows as he looked her over.

"Sonora? What the hell?"

She glanced at her phone then up at him, totally confused for a moment before amusement struck. "Well, I sure hope I get that quick a response the next time I text."

He closed the door behind him, crouching slightly because the roof of the tree house was shorter than his six-foot-two frame. "What are you doing here?"

His gaze darted around the eight-by-eight-foot space even as she rocked up to her knees and reached for his hand. "Waiting to give you your birthday present."

She tugged, and the unexpected move dropped him to his knees on the air mattress beside her, rocking slightly as he fought for balance.

"*Sonora.*"

He lost the battle when she pushed on his shoulder then moved quickly to straddle his hips. Smiling down, she took in the surprise and the heat rising in his eyes. "I know. You're having a birthday party with your friends. Far be it from me to disturb you."

His hands rested on her hips, and his expression turned to amusement. "The fact you're here, with what seems to be a bed and questionable intentions, is the straight-up definition of disturbing me."

Sonora pressed her hands to Ashton's chest, leaning over him and letting her hair fall around her face as she eased closer. Closer, until her lips just brushed his. "*Questionable* intentions? I'd hope they were pretty clear."

He slid a hand up her back to tangle his fingers in her hair. One small tug and he'd adjusted the angle so he could kiss her. Lips firm against hers as he took control. The heat between them as intense and quick to rise as always.

A moment later, he rolled them.

Sonora looked up at the man who meant so much to her yet still stood on the other side of some unfathomable line. They would find a way to get past it, but right now, they had a deadline to meet.

"Happy birthday, cowboy. Let's ride."

3

ASHTON

Ashton paused at the bottom of the stairs. He took a couple of deep breaths before returning to the party that was still in full swing. The mirror in the hallway showed him an expression on his face that was far more relaxed than an hour ago.

A man who had just been gifted something unexpected but deliciously fine.

"There you are." Gary shuffled down the stairs, a twinkle in his eyes as he juggled fistfuls of empty beer bottles. "I finally got the pool table away from the kids. You ready to lose some money?"

"It's my birthday. You know I'm going to kick your ass," Ashton returned as he reached to help with Gary's load before he dropped something.

Gary bantered back. The two of them were upstairs amongst the loud, raucous gathering in no time. There were no questions about where Ashton had been for the past hour, the party having carried on just fine without him.

It was a birthday to remember. Even losing soundly to Gary and James couldn't put a damper on Ashton's evening.

When it came time to say good night, Ashton pulled his nephew in for a hug then patted him firmly on the back. "It was the darnedest idea but turned out to be a blast."

"There's always a fun time to be had around the Ryder household," Josiah said as he marched up to say good night as well. For one second, Ashton wondered if the young man had an idea what exactly had been going on in the backyard of the Ryder household.

Only there was nothing but an innocent smile on Josiah's face when Ashton shook his hand. "Appreciate it."

"Anytime."

Ashton headed back out in the cold and climbed into the truck beside his friend. They grinned at each other like kids before Gary put the truck in gear and headed home. Back to the ranch where Ashton had deep roots and good family.

They were nearly back at Ashton's place when Gary broke the silence. "You going to see Sonora sometime soon?"

An image of her from earlier that evening rose, her hair spread on the pillow, cheeks rosy, lips swollen from his kiss. "Sometime."

His friend made a low noise. "Fine. I know you don't want to talk about it. But someday, Stewart, you're going to need to make a decision about what you're doing with that woman. And I hope you make it a smart one."

Ashton stared out the window as the lights of Silver Stone reflected off the snowy ground and created a landscape of stars on every level. It was somewhere beautiful, somewhere that had been home for a long, long time.

Somewhere that was still missing...*something.*

Someone?

A decision about what he was doing with Sonora? Seemed Ashton had been trying to make that one for over fifteen years.

A smart move? This coming year, he sure the hell was going to try.

I F YOU'D LIKE to find out how Ashton and Sonora's story concludes, **A RANCHER'S CHRISTMAS KISS** is the final book in the Holidays in Heart Falls series.

MISCHIEF AT THE FIRE HALL

Girls' night out always involves laughter and friendship, but this go-round, there are last-minute changes. Because of extreme freezing temperatures, Madison Zhao's baby shower gets combined with the guys hosting their own gathering at the fire hall. The final result is a surprise for Ryan that he'll never forget.

Featuring: Madison, Ryan and Madison's baby bump. Also most of the characters from the Holidays in Heart Falls series, plus Ginny Stone, Tucker Stewart, and Luke and Kelli Stone.)

Timeline: This story is set almost immediately after **A Cowboy's Christmas List.**

MADISON

December 29, Heart Falls

Not even a minute into the video, laughter bubbled up between the friends, but Madison waved it down. "Shoot. Who got the list of what we need? Brooke, did you write that down? Hanna?"

"Backing up." Yvette slid the mouse over the keyboard and rewound the YouTube video slightly. "Ready?"

Brooke lifted her pen as if it were a sword. "Mischief about to be managed."

Yvette hit Play, and the four women all leaned forward eagerly to watch the how-to video.

"Pre-plastered gauze. Applying it to unbroken body parts. I can see this project triggering all sorts of future trouble." Hanna turned a pale pink.

"Plus petroleum jelly. Or cocoa butter. *Hmmm.*" Madison bit her bottom lip to stop from making a dirty comment.

Thankfully, Brooke was more than willing to go there on

her behalf. "You realize, at this point, the guys would say they should be able to join in. Make their *own* body molds. Although, I doubt they'd suggest their *belly* as the body part in question. Ahem."

Snickers bounced around the room.

Madison and her friends were preparing for their monthly girls' night out, which this month became a joint outing and pre-baby celebration. And while she was excited as anything for the arrival of her baby sometime in the next couple of weeks, Madison really wanted the gathering to be for *all* of them, not her as the center of attention.

Still, she did have a very Madison-centric request that everyone could appreciate. Which was why her friends were even now helping research and plan for a fun, memorable event.

"Ladies make casts of their bellies and breasts. Guys make casts of their co—" The word vanished under Yvette's giggles. "Picturing this in my head is dangerous."

Brooke kept watching, reading through the directions. "Says after we apply the strips to the torso, it takes twenty to thirty minutes to fully dry." Her brows went up. "I wonder. Can a guy keep it up for that long without any further...*attention*?"

Her grin was contagious. "You're so bad," Madison snickered.

"Need anything in here?" Madison's husband, Ryan, poked his head around the corner into the baby's room, where the women were gathered.

Yvette pressed a hand to her mouth. Hanna's cheeks brightened to deep pink.

Only Brooke maintained her cheeky grin. "We should ask Ryan our burning question. He might know."

"Know what?" Ryan asked in all innocence.

"Never mind," Madison said with a laugh, pushing Brooke's shoulder. "You're terrible."

"She is terrible, but we love her." Ryan looked amused. "I should know better than to step into the room when I'm outnumbered. Come back to the living room when you're ready. The girls are nearly done making the first batch of cookies."

"We won't be too much longer," Madison assured him, blowing a kiss his direction.

It took a few minutes for two of them to make the shopping list, while the other two sent texts to get a tentative head count of who wanted to join the event.

"We've got a yes from Kelli, Rose, and Tansy. Ginny says maybe." Hanna handed over the list.

"Materials for eight, then." Brooke nodded. "I'm in Calgary tomorrow. Mack and I will grab everything we need."

Hanna looked a little worried. "You think we can all do a cast on the same day? It's going to take some room, and from the sounds of it, things could get messy, so this isn't a living room activity."

Brooke waved a hand. "We're meeting Sunday afternoon this time, so we can use the car shop. It's pretty empty this time of year, so I'm sure my dad won't mind. I'll hang some old curtains over the windows to make it perfectly private."

Madison laughed as she joined the rest of them in the kitchen, the warm scent of peanut butter cookies making her mouth water. She walked slowly, the heavy weight of her baby-full belly dragging lower than usual. "Privacy would be good, considering we plan to strip down to our skivvies and layer ourselves with plaster."

Her daughter by choice, Talia, came rushing up. "Hugs for the baby," the twelve-year-old insisted.

Madison stood still and allowed herself to be wrapped in her preteen's arms. She laid her hand on the girl's head and smiled as Talia leaned down to whisper at her belly. Talia had started the habit right after hearing she was going to be a big sister, and Madison had to fight tears of happiness every time it happened.

The rest of the time passed quickly before her friends were headed out the door with promises to chat and lots of excitement for the actual meetup on January second.

Only, when Sunday morning arrived, Ryan wore a far-too-concerned expression at the breakfast table. "Honey, I don't want to ruin your fun, but the weather has officially taken a turn for the worse."

She'd been watching out the window. The previous day, snow had fallen softly for hours, pretty as anything. Before they'd headed to bed, fresh snow lay in thick sheets over their backyard, piling up on the fence posts like mini haystacks.

Now the wind whipped in circles, whiteout conditions covering the entire south of Alberta. "We're not going to be outside. We'll be okay."

He shook his head. "Mack and I were talking last night when the temperature dropped so suddenly. The shop won't be warm enough for you gals to be stripping down and sticking gluey strips on yourself. Not without risking someone getting sick."

Disappointment rushed in. "I guess I'll have to do something else with my friends. You'll have to help me, though, because I really do want a belly cast while I'm big and glowing. And hopefully those days are numbered."

He leaned in and kissed her. "You're always beautiful and glowing, and of course, I'd help you. But I have another suggestion. Mack and I checked with Brad, and he said you can use the fire hall for girls' day out. Upstairs in the common area. It'll be warm, there are easy-to-wash floors, and everyone knows how to get there." His eyes sparkled with the tease.

Hope rushed back in. "Thank you for taking care of us. I'm so glad we can go ahead."

He waggled his brows at Talia. "What I didn't tell your mom

is that while she's spending time with her friends, you get to spend time with yours. Want to go to the fire hall with us?"

Talia cheered excitedly.

"You're going too?" Madison was struck with a sudden image of the rather risqué plaster cast Brooke had suggested and had to fight back a grin.

He gave her *a look*. "It's nearly negative forty, and that's before we add the wind chill. I'm not letting you go *anywhere* without me. Call me a caveman, but if you want this to happen right now, I'm your designated driver."

"Fine." His contented sigh was worth capitulating for.

"Mack's driving Brooke. And Brad's bringing Hanna and the kids. Alex says he and Yvette will swing by Buns and Roses to grab the sisters. And Ginny—well, I don't know which of them will actually drive, but Tucker says he, Luke, and Kelli will be there as well, plus they're bringing Emma to play with Talia."

Madison laughed. "So what you're saying is you're having a *guys'* gathering today. With the kids, yes?"

"With the kids," he assured her. "They'll stick with us, and you ladies will have all the privacy you want."

It was a wonderful solution.

As they got ready to head out early in the afternoon, she could hardly fault him for his caution. Her winter coat didn't close around her belly anymore, and when he backed their minivan out of the garage, the wind outside screamed loud enough to set her nerves jangling.

The inside of the fire hall was warm and a familiar setting for most of them. Madison left her husband and daughter behind on the main level of the hall, the other children already playing beside one of the trucks.

The volunteer firefighters on duty grinned and waved as she passed, but most were more focused on a puzzle laid out on the table. Only one of them rose and came over to say hello.

Charity Gruzing winked cheerfully. "Have fun. If we do get

a callout, you guys are fine to stay and finish up. Brad assured me there are enough extra bodies in the place, so you relax and enjoy yourself."

"Thanks. I'm glad to hear it." Madison offered the package she'd put together at home. "Here. As a thank-you for giving up your comfy space to us. I made you cookies."

Charity licked her lips and hummed appreciatively. "We'll just keep this a secret between us, right?"

"You hiding goodies from us?" The amused shout rang out from one of the other volunteers. "Thanks, Maddy."

"Thank *you*," Madison said over her shoulder as she made her way into the back room.

A cheer went up.

All her friends were already assembled, and Madison did her best to move smoothly forward to join them. Her attempt wasn't very successful. It felt as if the baby had changed position since that morning, and the only way forward was to walk like a cowboy who'd been in the saddle for days.

Brooke and Yvette burst into wide grins, glancing at each other before gesturing Madison to the chair of honour. The one decorated with balloons and streamers.

"Sit, and we'll get you a drink," Brooke commanded, still smiling widely.

Madison gave her the evil eye. "You were talking about my waddle, weren't you?"

"Yes," Brooke admitted. "Because I have never seen anyone make a waddle look as cute as you do. Not even Hanna when she was pregnant with Drew."

"It's the truth," Hanna said. "I'm so short, I looked as if I were ready to tip over at any moment. Brad kept threatening to duct tape pillows around my entire body."

Brooke nodded. "As for me, I fully expect to lumber like an elephant. Which will not be cute."

Amused, Madison watched and chatted while her friends

cut the pre-plastered strips into sections. She enjoyed a plate of goodies Tansy brought her but turned down the juice. "If we're going to do the plaster business soon, I'm not drinking. I already have to pee every five minutes."

"Then take a pit stop, and we'll get started." Ginny clapped her hands. "We're working in teams. Tarps and sheets are all in place, and Tansy and I will get the water set up."

Madison came back from the bathroom and settled in her chair. Hanna, Ginny, and Rose were also in the first round, the four chairs placed with backs toward the middle.

"Privacy, but we can still talk." Hanna dipped her chin. "I like it."

While Madison didn't particularly care if everyone saw her belly, they were doing full-torso casts, which meant stripping off their bras at some point. If it meant all of them were more comfortable, back-to-back was fine with her.

Her belly tightened, the baby pushing up in protest.

Yvette smiled as she knelt beside Madison's chair. "They're wiggly today."

"I just hope they don't plant both feet on my ribs and tap dance again. Or on my bladder," Madison said.

"Let's get going. Since we do have your bladder as a timer to beat."

They covered her belly with a thick layer of petroleum jelly before Yvette started. The water was warm, and every strip she laid in a crosshatch pattern over Madison's belly tingled briefly.

The baby wiggled some but mostly seemed pinned in place, especially as the cast immediately began to harden.

"This feels very weird," Rose shared. "Like I have volunteer abdominal muscles kicking into gear."

"It reminds me of Braxton-Hicks contractions," Hanna said.

"Yup." Madison twisted her head toward where Brooke was working on Hanna's cast. Brooke was all of fourteen weeks pregnant. "You are going to love those. I've been having them for the past two weeks. I've offered to let Ryan play the drums on me, my stomach gets so tight. Like an involuntary sit-up on overdrive."

The fire alarm went off, and Madison tensed.

"Breathe, sweetie," Yvette warned. "Kelli, you want to go see what's happening before our baby mama crawls out of her skin?"

"No prob." Kelli laid a hand on Ginny's shoulder. "Stop trying to put on the strips yourself. I'll be right back."

The alarm cut off a moment after Kelli left the room.

Madison took a deep breath and let it out slowly. "Charity did say they have full staff on tonight, so we're fine to keep going."

"Definitely," Yvette said. "Ready for the next step—so don't look. I'm doing your boobs."

Madison and the rest snickered, and activity resumed. Especially when Kelli darted back in and returned to work as well. "The guys said things are fine. The pumper truck's been called out to an accident on the highway. No casualties, but a tanker slid off the road into the ditch. The tow trucks want backup in case something goes wrong."

Still dangerous, but a controlled situation was better than a straight-up fire. "Sending good thoughts to all of them out on the call," Madison said softly.

The music in the background picked up again, and less than five minutes later, announcements began.

"We're done," Tansy said. "Rose doesn't have as much belly as Madison. Oh, and not as much boobs, either."

"You're a pain in the tushie," Rose muttered, but she laughed. "Turn my chair around so I can see everyone as I dry."

"Nearly finished," Kelli called out. "Ginny has three times the boobs of Rose."

"You're trouble, pure and simple," Ginny offered her sister-in-law. "I have *four* times more, if you want to be accurate."

"My poor boobies are feeling attacked," Rose offered.

"Good thing you've got armour for them." This from Hanna as Brooke rotated her chair.

The four of them currently covered in plaster glanced at each other, and laughter rang around the room. White plaster covered them from hips to collarbones, dips and bumps in vastly different sizes on display.

"You guys look amazing," Yvette insisted. "And yes, you're all built very differently, but the differences are beautiful. Way to celebrate the human body."

Madison agreed completely. The plaster was cooling, and it now felt as if she had a turtle shell on her abdomen and chest. She peered over the roundness of her belly at Brooke. "We're going to have to do you again when you're close to delivery."

"That will make for a neat comparison." The other woman glanced at her watch. "Snacks, anyone? You can't move much, but you can nibble on cookies."

Only, when the tray was offered to Madison, she turned it down. She wasn't sure if it was the momentary adrenaline rush from the alarm going off or if it was just one of those pregnancy things, but she didn't have an appetite anymore.

In fact, the cast drying on her belly was getting extremely uncomfortable. Enough so that she was regretting having the idea in the first place.

"How much longer?" she asked Yvette quietly as the girls continued to chat.

Yvette eyed her. Concern swept in, and she laid a hand on the cast and then knocked lightly. "I think we can take it off. I'll work carefully."

Madison waved off the offer to turn the chair. She just wanted the plaster off, *now*.

Yvette loosened the edges and pulled, the hard surface releasing easily from Madison's body as the jelly did its job.

Her friend wrapped a towel around Madison as she spoke quietly. "You okay?"

With one hand pushed to the tight surface of her belly, Madison worked to breathe evenly.

Dear Lord, what was wrong with her? She was on the edge of tears. As if she'd been abandoned in a broken-down shack in the middle of the storm instead of sitting in a warm room with her friends, doing body crafts and enjoying holiday treats. Words escaped, all mopey and lost. "I want Ryan."

"Sure. I can get him. You okay if I mention to Brooke that we need to adjust plans?"

Madison glanced at her friends. The other three who'd been wrapped up in strips were getting peeled out of their casts, laughter muted as they glanced her direction. Worry on their faces.

"I'm sorry," she said a little louder so they could all hear. "I'm... Something is wrong."

Instant motion. As if she'd announced she was about to explode, everyone headed in different directions. The three women now wrapped in towels dashed toward the shower room. Brooke took off at a sprint into the main fire hall. Kelli and Tansy moved the body casts to a safe position on the chairs against the wall then rolled the rest of the tarps and sheets out of the way.

Which was good, because Brooke must have flown downstairs. Before Madison could feel bad for making a fuss over nothing, Ryan burst into the room, Mack and Brad on his heels.

2

RYAN

Thirty minutes earlier

O f course, they'd had a callout. The one night Ryan really hoped the fire hall would stay quiet, it didn't happen. But that's how life seemed to work—roll with the punches and play with the hand you're dealt.

He and Brad gathered Talia and the other children at the side of the room, staying out of the way as the team on call took off like a well-oiled machine, Alex riding shotgun.

The kids rallied quickly, back to their hopscotch and climbing games, burning off energy in the way only children powered by potato chips and fruit juice could.

Brad pulled himself out of playing and leaned on the wall next to Ryan. "How're you doing?"

"Hoping we don't get any more calls tonight, or we'll be pulling straws to see who suits up." Ryan checked his watch. He figured another hour at the most before he could casually wander upstairs to check on Maddy. Not going was driving him wild. He just had this strange feeling…

"Wasn't talking about the emergency lineup," Brad drawled. He met Ryan's questioning gaze. "How are you dealing with things in terms of being ready for baby day?"

"I have done this before," Ryan said dryly before grinning sheepishly. "Which means my sleep is nearly as messed up as Madison's, and I'm scared to death even while I pretend everything's going to be fantastic and all smooth sailing."

Brad let out a heavy sigh. "Yeah. That's what I figured." He rested a commiserating hand on Ryan's shoulder for a moment. Then he chuckled evilly. "Well, if we do have any emergency callouts that involve babies over the next months, we need to wrangle it so Mack has to go as backup. With Brooke up to bat after Madison, he needs more experience with deliveries."

"I heard that," Mack called, passing the ball in his hands back to Brad's son.

Drew raced after it.

The three little girls in the room followed like sheepherders, and he was their lone sheep.

Mack slipped in close. "Babies don't scare me," he assured them. "Got nearly a dozen births under my belt. I mean, assists. Hell if I could handle the actual work."

"They scare the hell out of me," Tucker said. "Babies and toddlers, I mean. I like them when they're older and have attitudes and brainpower."

"Trust me, babies have brainpower," Brad told him. "Drew knew exactly which cry to pull on Hanna and which on me. Kid had us hopping to his wishes within hours of popping out of the chute."

Luke looked thoughtful. "Don't know that I've ever thought about a favourite age for kids. My nieces were just always there, it seems. Every stage, there was something I liked. Then the rest of them arrived. They're all so different but great in their own ways."

"You and Kelli going to start a family soon?" Brad asked.

Luke grinned. "Maybe."

"Seriously?" Shocked widened Tucker's eyes. "Oh, damn, that's not good."

Luke frowned. "Why?"

"If you guys start, then everyone will be looking at Ginny and me." Tucker looked a touch panicked for a minute. He narrowed his gaze. "You're bullshitting. You're trying to make me *think* you're going to go for it, but then you won't."

"Life is not a competition," Ryan said dryly.

"Speak for yourself." Luke and Tucker spoke at the exact same moment, both suddenly very intent on staring daggers at each other.

Well, that was interesting.

Ryan decided to poke. "So, does this mean you're both going to try to convince your women it's time to get things rolling?"

"Mayb—"

"Ryan." Brooke appeared at the top of the stairs, her shout ringing over them and cutting all teasing short. "Get up here, now. Mack, Brad, you too. I think Madison's in labour."

A rush of adrenaline hit, and Ryan took off without a backward glance. He trusted his friends to keep his daughter safe while he went to Madison's aid.

"Go, guys, Luke and I have got the kids." Tucker's voice faded in the distance as Ryan hit the top of the stairs.

Footsteps pounded behind him, but Ryan didn't stop until he had burst into the common room. He spotted Madison seated on a chair, towel around her shoulders.

He dropped beside her and pulled her into his arms. "Hey, honey. What's up?"

She had tears in her eyes, and worry covered her usually happy face. "I don't feel very good."

"The baby?"

Yvette was there, her hand resting on Madison's knee. "She let me take a quick peek. I think the baby's crowning."

"But I'm not in labour," Madison insisted. She pressed her hands to her belly. "Or it's a weird labour. It's like Braxton-Hicks, but my muscles won't stop squeezing. I've tried to relax, but it's not working."

Brad squatted beside Madison's chair. "Hey, sweetie. You okay if I take over medical assistance? Let Ryan hold your hand, and I'll see where your baby is at."

"Okay," Madison agreed even as she glanced up at Yvette. "You stay too. Please?"

"Of course." Yvette squeezed Madison's knee. "I'm your backup. Everyone here loves you, and we'll all help however we can."

Which made some of the panic drilling through Ryan ease. Only a little, though, because *damn*. Having the baby early, in the middle of a whiteout, was not on the agenda.

He should have known, though, that as with all emergencies, his friends would come through. Plus, being at the fire hall with trained EMTs and first-aid providers was not a bad place to be during a medical crisis.

Brad gave Madison a quick examination, wonder on his face as he nodded at Yvette. "You're really close to delivery, Maddy. Not quite there, but close."

"Too close to get to the hospital?" Ryan asked.

A quick shake of Brad's head. "By the time we drive there, the baby might arrive."

"I don't want to have my baby in an emergency transport in these temperatures." Madison frowned. "But I'm *not* in labour."

"Yes, you are," Brad informed her quietly. "Really. Every woman feels labour pains differently, but you're dilated to nearly ten centimeters."

She squirmed upright. "I need to stand up."

Ryan pulled her to her feet, and Madison breathed out slowly as she caught her balance. She glanced around the room. "Well, there goes girls' night out."

Yvette laughed. "They're fine with the kids for a bit. The girls had showers—do you want to have one? Wash off the plaster goo and relax a little more?"

A quick glance at Brad followed. "Can I do that?" Madison asked.

"If Ryan stays beside you to help with your balance, sounds like a great idea." Brad nodded at Yvette. "We should get you in training for humans."

"No way. I hear they bite." She pulled a pile of clothes into her arms and tilted her head toward the shower room. "I've got your clothes. Put something on you feel comfy in from the waist up when you're done. It'll mean juggling fewer towels."

A moment later they were in the privacy of the shower room. Ryan stripped down as well, standing under the warm spray with Madison leaning against his chest.

She stared up at him. "Hey. I guess we're having a baby today."

"I guess we are." He kissed her softly then went back to rubbing the soap in circles over her belly and sides. "Let's get you cleaned up first, just in case."

"Sounds smart. You're a keeper, you know that?" She tilted her head back and let the water pour over her face as he took care of her.

She was so beautiful. His fingers shook, he was scared to death, but his heart was so full at that moment, he didn't think he could contain it.

"I love you," he whispered.

Her eyes opened, and she smiled, mischief all over her expression. "Good."

A laugh burst free. He washed her, dried her, then helped

her put on his button-down shirt instead of her own stuff. It just felt...right.

They walked the common room for a bit after escaping the shower. Their friends came and chatted, including Brooke.

"You may as well stick around," Madison offered. "You'll be doing some version of this soon enough."

"Can I have the no-labour version of this labour thing? That would be cool," Brooke teased. She squeezed Maddy in a quick hug. "I'd be honoured to be here."

Barely an hour later, Madison once again froze, her face contorting as she glanced around frantically. "Umm, something changed."

The next few minutes passed in a blur. Her water broke, and Madison's groans turned into gasps as pain suddenly kicked in.

Someone had brought in a mattress from the bunkhouse. That's where Ryan sat with Madison braced against him as she brought their son into the world.

Brad's grin was ear to ear when he passed the baby to Yvette. She carefully wiped the newborn clean, working around his outstretched arms and his indignant shrieks. "Everything looks good. You're amazing, Madison."

"She's a miracle," Ryan said, his heart in his throat as he waited for Yvette to finish. He pressed his lips to Maddy's cheek. "He's perfect."

Madison offered a watery smile. "I'm going to cry," she calmly announced.

Then she did. Soft, deep gasps that sent Ryan's gut into worried knots. At least until he looked into her eyes as Yvette handed over the swaddled baby.

Maddy might be crying, but there was joy at the heart of it.

"Congratulations." Yvette again. "You did great. And so did baby Zhao. Good lungs on this one."

"That's all Ryan's side of the family," Madison joked, wiping her eyes with the back of her hand as she stared at her baby. "Hi, sweetie. I'm glad you're here, even if you have to work on your calendar skills. Welcome to our family."

"Our family, and more," Ryan murmured. He traced a finger along one soft cheek as Madison moved the baby into position to nurse. Teeny lips pursed, rooting instinct pushing him into the perfect position to latch on.

Silence fell as, for one brief moment, everyone stared in wonder, considering the miracle they'd gotten to witness.

Maybe babies arrived every day. Maybe it was natural and something that had happened since the beginning of time.

That didn't make today any less miraculous.

They waited until Madison was cleaned up and dressed to bring in Talia and the rest of their friends.

Talia crawled up on the couch next to Madison, laying her cheek against her mom's, staring with a dropped jaw at her baby brother.

"I asked for a brother," Talia confessed softly. She looked up at Madison. "I know they're louder than sisters, but you have such good little brothers, I wanted to have one too."

Madison laughed, curling her free arm around their daughter and kissing her gently. "You're going to be an awesome big sister. I know it. I couldn't be happier."

"I could be," Tansy teased. She sat next to Rose, arms around each other as their friends all waited for their turn to hold the baby. "I want to know his name, since I doubt you're following through on that promise you gave me in December. *Tansy* is a great name and all, but he looks as if he needs something a little different."

"Ryan? You want to do the honours?" Madison asked sweetly.

Her smile was back in full force as he slid next to her to hold all three of them. His wife, his daughter, and his son.

Looking out into the crowd—made up of so many people he cared deeply about—Ryan nodded.

"This is Justin. Because we want to remember the past and celebrate a future full of love."

A gentle cheer went up. "To Justin."

"Welcome, baby."

"You're going to be very happy."

A multitude of well-wishes rang out, but Ryan had returned to staring at his son. At Madison, who was his best friend forever and the owner of his heart.

He leaned toward her, kissing Talia in passing. Kissing Justin.

Kissing Madison before whispering with everything in him, "I love you. All of you, so much."

"Good," Madison said again, making him grin.

Brooke brought a very belly-full cast forward, winking at Maddy. "I'll take charge of this. You've got a few other things to take care of right now, so if you trust me, I'll bring it over once it's sanded and primed."

"Thanks, hon," Madison said.

"I loved that I got to see Justin being born." Brooke kissed her cheek, "Thank you."

The group took turns saying goodbye until it was down to Yvette, Brad, and Hanna in the back room.

"Talia can sleep over with us for the night, if she wants. We'll stop at your place to pick her up so she can grab her things," Hanna offered. "Also, we're following you home to make sure *you* get there safely. Because I need to."

They all laughed, but Ryan understood.

"If you want, I'll come over and finish setting things up, since Justin was early. In fact, let me head over there right now, and I'll get some supper started." Yvette waved off their thanks. "Alex isn't done with his shift for hours, and I'd love to be a help."

Brad found an infant car seat in the storage for them to use to get home. Bundling up the tiny bit of humanity and preparing to leave felt unreal. It was strange to go from the noise and energy of the gathering to just the four of them in the warmed-up car. Madison, Ryan, Talia, and Justin.

Justin, who had been no more than a bump when they'd started out that afternoon.

Madison stared at Ryan in the rearview mirror from her perch in the backseat next to the baby. "Does it get any less amazing?"

"Never," he assured her.

"Good."

Her new favourite word. He grinned.

Then mischief flashed in her eyes. "You'll be happy to know I ordered matching sweaters for all of us for our family portrait this spring. I can't wait for you to see them."

Laughter escaped. Ryan could only imagine what she'd found for them to wear. But he'd wear it, happily. Because that's the kind of joy Madison brought into his world.

He took his family home, a convoy of cars and trucks following behind, because *everyone* wanted to be sure they were okay. It was like an impromptu parade through Heart Falls. Bringing home his expanded family.

Bringing home love.

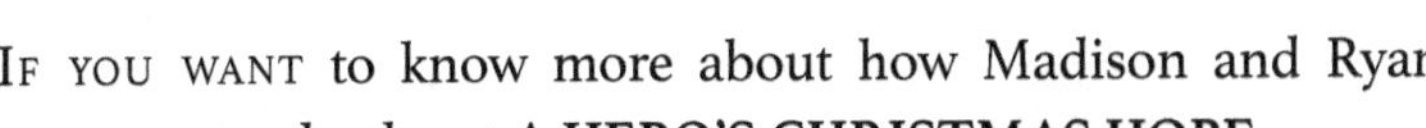

IF YOU WANT to know more about how Madison and Ryan's story starts, check out **A HERO'S CHRISTMAS HOPE.**

SHARING SECRETS

Girls' night out is getting a little wild. When it's late, and the tequila is flowing, that's when the secrets come out. One-night stands? It appears a few of the ladies have indulged over the years, including a few surprises...

Featuring Rose and Tansy Fields, Sydney Jeremiah (the new doctor in town), and Petra Sorenson (sister to Zach from *The Cowgirl's Chosen Love*), plus a lot of tequila. Oops?

Timeline: This story takes place after the other vignettes in this collection, and early during **A Forever Family**.

1

ROSE

March, Heart Falls.

L ater, Rose would call it *Girls' Night Out Gone Wrong*.

The day had begun as usual, with both she and her sister Tansy working Buns and Roses, the café and flower/knickknack shop they owned together. Rose snuck away for an appointment with the bank in the afternoon, and the eye-opening discussion had set her buzzing with excitement.

She'd barely had time to share the details with Tansy of how and what was possible in terms of making their shop even bigger and better when the first of their friends arrived at five, arms laden with food for a potluck.

Sometimes girls' night out involved a project; sometimes it was just a gathering for food, fun, and kindred spirits. And drinking—

Two hours later, it appeared drinking was the night's featured activity.

Rose lifted her glass and accepted a top-up on her

margarita. "Your dip is dangerous, Petra. I love nacho chips to start, and then you had to bring that decadent, calorie-laden offering."

Petra Sorenson was visiting her brother Zach and had come along with her sister-in-law Julia for the night out. She made her way from the kitchen back to the gathering and placed a second steaming bowl of spicy, cheesy goodness on a trivet. "You're welcome. But seriously, there's no calories. All veggies."

"Because...cheese is somehow a *vegetable*?" Tansy inquired.

"Cheese comes from milk that comes from cows, and cows eat grass, and *that's* a vegetable," Petra said brightly. "Yes?"

"Dear Lord, please say that around my brother-in-law," Kelli Stone said with a snicker. "The man is wonderful, but that's the kind of thing that would make Caleb lose his shit."

"Our guys are usually hard to rile up," Karen said, nodding slowly. "But that one might get Finn as well."

Kelli grinned. "You know, they all think part of what we do on these nights out is share ways to torment them."

"It's a good idea." Tansy nodded. "I approve. Anyone have new suggestions for ways to torment our men?"

"You don't have a man," Rose pointed out. "Neither do I."

Tansy lifted a finger in the air. "Ah, but we do. We have our father, who is the most delightful of men to tease. It's only right after the way he treated us throughout our teen years. Coming to the door to meet our dates dressed in everything from a bathrobe to full knight's armor."

"Seriously?" Petra laughed. "I thought my dad was the only one who did that stuff."

"I assume it's in the Dad Handbook," Rose offered.

Petra's eye's flashed with amusement. "Speaking of tormenting the men in our lives, I thought my brother was going to faint this morning. I gave Julia some baby clothes and magazines I brought with me."

All eyes swung instantly to Julia. She flipped up her palms in protest. "No. To all your inquiring minds, *no*."

Petra shrugged. "I heard Madison had her baby, and my sisters had a ton of stuff for me to bring as hand-me-downs." Her grin widened evilly. "It was fun to freak Zach out, though. He stared at *What to Expect When You're Expecting* like it was a snake."

Like that, the conversation flipped into discussing what everyone was reading, and listening to, and had on hold at the library.

Rose sat contentedly, soaking it all in.

These women were more than just friends. They were her connections to Heart Falls and beyond, and while the composition of ladies changed on a monthly basis as people dealt with jobs and kids and families, they were always there for each other. It was something Rose could count on.

A blessing beyond imagining.

Around eight, phones started ringing, and the group quickly got a lot smaller.

"We're out of here."

Karen Marlette gathered their things as her sister Julia hurriedly explained, "Sorry. That was Zach. He and Finn decided they want to head out tonight so we'll be ready for the auction first thing in the morning."

Petra glanced up from the squishy old couch gracing Tansy and Rose's living room. She pushed back her long blonde hair then attempted to wiggle forward, the old couch clinging to her. "Hang on. I didn't know we were leaving. Give me a second, and I'll come with you."

Julia waved a hand. "Stay. We'll be back by tomorrow night. You came to Heart Falls specifically to have a holiday and relax. A full, uninterrupted girls' night out is exactly what you need to start your week with us."

"Agreed. You need to stay." Tansy leaned over Petra's shoulder to top up her peach margarita. "You're far too tense."

Petra snickered. "Hardly. Not after these drinks. How much alcohol is in them?"

"Enough that I'm officially done as well." Kelli Stone rose to her feet, teetered a few times, then grinned as she glanced around the room. "My man is picking me up, and I'm going to jump his very sexy cowboy bones. Might not even wait until we get home."

"Dangerous but fun." The comment came from a recent newcomer to their gatherings as she leaned forward and rested her elbows on her knees. Dr. Sydney Jeremiah had been quiet for a lot of the evening, but it was more like she was listening and soaking it all in than because she was too shy to participate.

She was a petite thing with deep-red hair and spectacular silver eyes. More than that, she had a supersharp brain and a killer attitude. She'd recently set up a medical practice in the Heart Falls area, and Rose was impressed by her on so many levels.

Sydney raised a brow. "You'll have to tell me sometime where the locals party."

"So you can find a partner and go parking?" Tansy moved aside to let Kelli join the others at the door.

"Always good to have options," Sydney offered with a wink.

After the flurry of goodbyes, it was down to the four of them: Tansy and Rose, Sydney and Petra.

Rose accepted a refill on her own glass then settled in the chair next to the couch. She momentarily glared at Tansy when her sister propped her feet on the coffee table, then decided to ignore her. For the next four hours, they all laughed, drank, and shared stories.

Petra might not be local, but she'd visited enough over the past couple of years that she'd become a solid part of their girl gang. She had the room in stitches, sharing stories about growing up with her big family and her brother Zach's attempts to deal with being the only boy in a family of six.

"When I realized Zach was hiding on the balcony, ready to jump in and defend my virtue, I cued up a murder podcast and did a voice simulation adjustment so it would sound like me and my date. The podcast started with casual conversation then slipped between one breath and the next into knives, screaming, and mayhem. You should have seen Zach's face when he ripped open the screen door to charge in and save me only to find my date and I sitting on opposite sides of the room holding signs that said *gotcha*."

"Mean. Mean and wonderful." Tansy grinned evilly. "That's a neat techno trick."

Petra shrugged. "Computers like me. But that, my friends, is what happens when a big brother decides he needs to chaperone the only sister he's got who's younger than him."

"No overprotective brothers for us," Rose pointed out. "Four sisters."

"Lots of girl families repped here tonight. Five sisters in mine," Petra reminded them. She turned toward Sydney. "You?"

"Youngest of three girls. Also two older brothers, so yeah, there's been a bit of overprotectiveness at times. Especially considering we were all off at college and university a lot younger than usual." Sydney took a deep drink of her wine then eased back farther in her chair. "God, I needed this night. Thanks so much for including me."

"You are very welcome," Rose said sincerely. "You've been working hard. I've heard nothing but good things about the clinic."

"Good. I love being in charge and the change in scenery, no matter how much work it's been." Sydney inclined her head toward Tansy and Rose. "You guys obviously love running Buns and Roses."

"It's the second-best thing in my life. Or third," Tansy teased. "Depending on where I rank chocolate that day."

Rose laughed, that contented sensation inside only building. "We do love it, and it's going great. So well that expansion plans are in the works."

"Good for you," Petra said with deep approval before she focused her attention on her glass and took a long drink. She smacked her lips, happiness sliding in hard on her face as she added, "I'm branching out as well."

"More accounting tech programs?" Rose asked.

"Hacking," Petra offered airily before they all exploded into guffaws of amusement.

More conversation followed, and more drinking, until Rose considered cutting herself off before she couldn't make it down the hall to her own bedroom.

"You guys are staying the night," Tansy announced. She'd returned from her bedroom with a pile of blankets she dropped on their sprawled bodies. "We all passed legal driving limits hours ago."

Sydney nodded then eyed Petra. "You get the floor. You'd never fit on the couch."

"You can bunk with me," Tansy offered. "Rose only has a twin mattress, but I have a king, so there's room for us both."

Petra dipped her chin regally before turning her tipsy smile on Rose's sister. "I accept your generous offer. But I should clarify that I am sadly as far to the het side as they come, so having only one bed will not lead to...how would Lisa say it? Oh, right. *Shenanigans!*"

Tansy laughed. "Your virtue is safe, even without your brother leaping in like Kool-Aid man."

"Okay, then." A huge dramatic sigh escaped Petra, her smile wide. "No one-night stand for us."

"You ever do that? Have a one-night stand?" Sydney stared

into her wine, a pleased smirk on her lips that hinted at what her answer would be.

A snicker sounded on Rose's left. "You look like a cat who not only got into the cream but one who caught a mouse and then commandeered the best seat in the house." Tansy leaned in close. "If we're going to confess all our sins, I think you should start."

"Not a sin." Petra hiccupped. "'Scuse me." She batted her lashes. "Well, not a sin if you do it right."

"And if *they* do it right." Sydney somehow smirked even harder.

"That means your answer is yes," Rose said. There were small flutters in her belly at the thought. But was it the thought of the sex or the fact it appeared all three of the other women in the room were ready to confess their adventures?

And she had nothing to share.

"Yes," Sydney admitted. "A few times." She frowned for a moment. "Wait. Strictly speaking, a couple means twice, so a few means three or four. Yes?"

"Makes sense."

Sydney nodded then narrowed her gaze as if thinking. "What's more than four?"

"A rock star." This from Tansy, who had put down her drink. "Also ballsy. Talk about dangerous, sweetie."

"I was always careful," Sydney insisted. "But I didn't want to date anyone officially while I was in school, especially since I was years too young for most of them. Besides, most of the people in my classes were just as exhausted as I was. Finding a good, healthy specimen to share one night with when I did have time and energy was emotionally and relationally simpler."

"Simple is good," Tansy agreed. "I had one night with a cowboy during Stampede years ago that, oh my *gawd*, made me tingle for days. But Rose and I were just setting up the shop here, and no way did I have time for anything more than some toe-curling entertainment."

Rose blinked at her sister. "I had no idea."

Tansy shrugged then grinned. "That means I did it right. Family is not supposed to know when you have a short-term fling. That's part of the *simple* equation."

Before Rose could respond, Petra interrupted. "Agreed." She leaned forward and covered her mouth for a moment before blurting, "I had a one-night stand the weekend Zach and Julia got hitched."

"Get out." Rose gaped at her. "*Here*? In Heart Falls?"

"Yup, but before you ask, not someone *from* Heart Falls." Petra was absolutely gloating now. "He was in town for…something. I didn't really ask because, hey-ho, he could dance. And then, when he took me to bed, he had this thing he did with his tongue, and—"

"Details later. Like never, later," Tansy insisted.

Rose took a deep breath. "I guess I've never had the right place or time or partner who inspired me to throw caution to the wind like that. I'm not opposed, but lightning has never struck," she admitted.

Sydney reached over and patted her leg. "Not a contest. Plus, just because the other kids are jumping off the bridge, it doesn't mean you have to as well."

"Exactly." It took Petra three tries to get the word out, and they were all giggling madly when she finally did. She nodded firmly at Rose. "It's not something you have to do, but if you want to do it, and the chance arises, why not?"

Drunken laughter and storytelling finally rolled to a stop somewhere around two a.m. when Tansy pulled Petra into her bedroom, a rumble of laughter drifting from them both.

The apartment fell quiet. Rose ignored the dirty glasses and half-empty chip bags on the coffee table. Instead, she grabbed a blanket to throw over Sydney, who was curled up on the couch.

The woman opened her eyes, looking far too alert considering all of them were more than three sheets to the wind. "Rose?"

"Yeah?"

Those shockingly silver eyes looked at her as if Sydney were seeing into Rose's very soul. "I meant what I said. I had my reasons to enjoy sex in casual situations. If it's not your thing, don't feel you need to."

"Right now, all I need to do is pass out and sleep for three days straight," Rose said.

"Good idea." Sydney nodded firmly then closed her eyes. "Or at least until ten, and then we'll drink lots and lots of strong coffee."

"I got you covered," Rose promised. Impulsively, she sat next to Sydney and offered a hug. "You're okay for a supersmart, wickedly determined woman."

Sydney snickered then accepted the connection, squeezing Rose tight. "And you're more than okay for a brilliantly talented woman with a kind heart and a generous soul."

Rose glowed as she crawled into her bed. Brilliantly talented. She liked that one.

She was nearly asleep when the thought drifted through her hazy mind.

Brilliant is good, but it might be fun to be impulsive, just one time.

A FOREVER FAMILY

For the past year, Ivy and Walker Stone have been working to expand their family. They've filled out forms until their fingers cramped, had home visits with social workers, and planned for the future. Walker and his brothers have done construction and renovations to his and Ivy's home in Heart Falls to make room for the coming new additions.

And now the day they've waited for is about to arrive.

Bonus... Tucker and Ginny's wedding is included in this story!

Timeline: Action begins in January after **A Rancher's Christmas Kiss.**

1

____

January 14, Heart Falls

Walker Stone leaned on the fence and gave the horse in the arena the barest hint of his attention. It wasn't that work was dragging...

Fuck it. This day felt like at least thirty-six hours and counting. He sighed while checking his watch as discreetly as possible.

The brotherly slap to the back of his head that followed said he'd been anything but successful in the attempt.

"We boring you?" Caleb growled as he stopped at Walker's side and glared.

"Sorry. Distracted there for a second." Walker worked to refocus. "I'm not sure this horse is worth the money or the time she'd cost us."

"Really? Luke said Barenaked Lady is right up our alley."

Walker blinked. He glanced at the horse then down to the paper in his hand. *Shit.* He'd lost his concentration more than a second ago according to this. They were at least a half dozen horses farther down the auction sheet than he'd expected. "Fuck. I missed a few. Yeah, this one's good."

Caleb rested his hands on Walker's shoulders. "Go outside. Call Ivy, get an update. Do whatever you need to screw your head on straight. We'll meet you at the truck in an hour."

"I can stay," Walker insisted.

"You need to go." Caleb glowered at him. "You're useless right now. I get that you need a distraction, but you're making me lose *my* concentration as well. One of us needs to keep his shit together."

Walker nodded, then amusement escaped. "I notice you aren't hoping Luke and Dustin are of sound enough mind to get this auction right without us."

"Dustin is busy flirting. Luke is plotting something with Kelli for next weekend, so he's nearly as bad as you."

"Unlikely," Walker admitted. He itched to touch base with Ivy, though, so he gave in. "Thanks. I'll make this up to you; I swear I will."

"Brother, you're waiting for one of the most precious things a man can have to arrive. I'm not mad, and I don't expect payback. But I do need you to get out," Caleb said dryly.

Walker got.

Outside, the bitter cold snapped at his skin. January in Alberta had followed her usual pattern, sliding into a hellish deep freeze for the past two weeks. The windchill only made it worse. A brilliant blue sky hung overhead, pretty as anything, without a cloud in sight. Shivering, he turned his collar up as he hurried away from the heated auction barn and back to his truck and trailer.

He waited until he had the engine going and heaters turned up high before he pulled out his phone.

No messages.

Walker checked his watch. Ivy should've been out of the

classroom and doing vice principal stuff now. Maybe phoning wouldn't be bad.

A loud ring sounded. Ivy was calling *him*.

Thank God.

"Hey, Snow."

"Hey, love. Am I interrupting?" she asked quickly.

"Hardly. Caleb kicked me out of the auction because my concentration is crap. All I want is to be home with you." He paused. "No, that's not *all* I want."

She sighed. "I know. No calls on my end, either. But soon. It's got to be soon."

"I keep thinking of our girls," he admitted softly.

After all the months of work and weeks of waiting, they'd been given a set of paperwork that included pictures of the sisters who were so close to being theirs. The girls also had an older brother, fathered by a different man. Carter was being cared for by his paternal grandmother, so while the children got to have regular visits with each other, only the girls were up for adoption.

The first time meeting the girls in person? It hadn't mattered that the dog in the yard next door to the foster home had barked the entire visit, the high-pitched sound scraping their nerves like speaker feedback. Walker had fallen in love.

Chloe was six years old. She'd held onto her four-year-old sister, Harper, as if protecting a priceless treasure. Both of them were on the thin side with dark brown hair and their souls in their eyes.

"They're too little to feel so lost. Their expressions knocked my feet out from under me and broke my heart," Walker admitted. "Not being able to scoop them up and bring them home with us is killing me."

"I know. When we met them, I wasn't sure if I should hug them or not," Ivy reminded him softly. "Then Harper leaned against my leg to look at the picture book we brought about horses. She was almost in my arms—"

Ivy broke off, tears choking her.

"I know. I know," he soothed. "Damn it, I should be home with you."

A soft but wet laugh answered him. "It wouldn't make me less weepy. You're supposed to be right where you are. Trying to work, same as me," Ivy told him. "We'll both be taking time off when they do arrive. We need to find a way to keep it together until that happens."

"Shall we invite our families over on Sunday to finish the playhouse?" Walker offered. "The women can cook up something hearty, and the guys and I will swing hammers."

"Sounds like the start of a plan. Maybe the women should swing the hammers, and you guys can do the cooking," she countered.

"Forecast calls for minus fifty with windchill," he informed her.

She snorted indelicately. "The fact I don't go out in that kind of weather doesn't mean my sisters wouldn't dive in wholeheartedly. How about we issue an open call to work and play? We'll order as much pizza for dinner as needed."

"Sounds great. Although I bet someone ends up baking cookies tomorrow."

"I'm not taking that bet," Ivy returned quickly.

"Because you know I'm right?"

She laughed softly. "Because sometime in the past, you must have won a bet against my sister Tansy. Every time she stops by, fresh cookies magically appear on the counter."

"I have no idea what you're talking about," he insisted.

Although it was true. At last tally, Tansy owed him another couple months' worth. He couldn't figure out how she could be so smart with everyone else and yet keep losing to him.

Part of him didn't want to know if she was secretly losing

just to make him feel good in a patented Tansy *love ya, bro* kind of way.

The sunshine outside was back in his heart. Just talking with Ivy, planning with her, dreaming and hoping and laughing—

It made the wait bearable.

"I love you so much," he told her quietly. "We'll just keep working to make the best home ever for our girls so it's ready when they are."

"I love you too," she said sweetly. "I'll call my grandma right now. I know she and Ashton can't be there, but she's been begging for updates."

"I'll message the rest of them," he promised.

The quiet after the call, with only the buzz of the heaters and rumble of the engine, soothed Walker with a solemn peace. Yes, it was hell to wait, but there was no way to change the timing. Until the final paperwork was done, Chloe and Harper had to wait too.

He opened his phone and wrote the invitation for the work bee, because while waiting might suck, waiting with his family was far better.

2

———————

"So this is where you're hiding."

Ivy glanced to the right as her mother swept into the quiet reading room. "I'm watching the action without having to face the cold or put in earplugs."

"They are vocal today, aren't they?" Sophie settled on the couch beside her daughter. "The last of the Stone crew just arrived. You married into a horde, my darling."

"A very polite horde at least," Ivy pointed out.

Sophie linked her fingers with Ivy's, and the two of them sat quietly for a moment, staring out the massive windows.

The original home Ivy had purchased was a tiny place. Too small for even just her and Walker. When they started the process of adoption, Walker had surprised her with an updated floor plan. One that kept the original house as a base then added two side arms with bedrooms for the children and playrooms and all the space a family could ask for.

The new kitchen now filled both the old kitchen and the old living room. The former primary bedroom had been transformed into a quiet reading nook that faced the backyard. With sliding doors to use during the summer, the room was bright and cheery and both a retreat and way to be part of the action in the backyard.

Which was currently a snowball fight, not playhouse construction. Thankfully, the weather had warmed to just above freezing, and those who weren't hurling snowballs were cheering enthusiastically from the sidelines. Even the horses tucked into the small arena Walker had added to the yard eyeballed the activity. They peeked out of their shelter briefly then shook their heads as if to say *people are odd*, retreating into the warmth of the small barn once again.

Gentle music played in the background of Ivy's retreat. Something classically Japanese. Her father must have taken control of the sound system again.

All the action and liveliness outside, the peace inside, and still a small flutter of panic rushed her. What if—

What if she couldn't do this? What if Chloe and Harper needed more than she had to give? What if—

"Hush, sweetheart." The hand pressed to her knee broke into her spinning thoughts. Her mother turned wise eyes toward her. "You're going to be okay."

Ivy let out a slow breath. "How do you do that? How do you always know?"

Sophie shrugged. "Sometimes it's because your tells give you away. Shoulders tightening, breath speeding up. But this time, you were about to break my fingers."

"Oh my God, I'm sorry."

Ivy tried to release her, but her mom kept her grip firm.

Sophie laid their joined hands in her lap. "You've managed to accomplish everything you've set your mind to. This is one more thing, darling. You're going to be exactly what those girls need."

"But I'm still *me*," Ivy said softly. "I'm still in here, not out there." She gestured with her free hand toward the chaos and happiness blooming outside the window. Pointing as her little sister Fern scooped up two-and-half-year-old Tyler Stone and spun him in a circle. The little boy's squeal of delight could be heard through the window. "I'm so much better than I was, but I'll never be the life of the party."

"No, thank goodness, because we already have Tansy, and between her and your father, there's more than enough partying going on around here." Sophie twisted on the seat to grasp both of Ivy's hands in her own. "When we went to pick you up from your foster home, I was terrified."

Ivy froze. "You were not."

The story of Ivy's adoption had been shared many times over the years, but that tidbit had never been a part of it before.

Her mother smiled, a soft, almost sad expression. "Oh, I know. I was also excited and worried and thrilled and content in a way I'd never been until then. Twenty-five years old, your father was twenty-eight, and we were so ready to have a family."

"Then suddenly you had a four-year-old who was delicate and frail—"

"And *perfect*," Sophie interrupted. "You were perfect. Yes, we spent a lot of time at hospitals. We spent a lot of time getting to know you and learning how to love you in ways that fit your quiet nature. That's who you were and what you brought to our family. We would have been very ungrateful and heartless people to expect you to be anything other than yourself."

"You've never been anything less than loving," Ivy assured her. "My first memories are of your smile. And you hugging me." She wrinkled her nose. "And Dad wearing some silly mask with tusks that was supposed to make me feel better about using an ordinary oxygen mask."

Sophie laughed. "Oh, the *mask*. Yes, that was a creative moment on his part."

Ivy nodded slowly. "But you were scared? To bring me home?"

"I wasn't scared about you. I knew you would be exactly

what we needed. You made us into a family, you see. And families? I could do that. Your grandmother had already turned herself, my father, and me into a family years before, so I had some idea of how building a family should go."

Grandmother Sonora, who had been only eighteen when she'd fallen in love with a widower, father to a nine-year-old daughter. Ivy considered her grandma a badass and loved her beyond measure.

"I was terrified you wouldn't love me," Sophie said softly.

Ivy shook her head in confusion. "I don't understand."

"See, up until then, everyone in my world was there because they'd chosen to be." Her mother lifted her shoulders in a gentle motion. "Your father and I chose to spend time together, which led to falling in love. Your grandmother chose me as a daughter. My friends, my work, my world—all the people I knew cared about me. They were all there because they'd decided, at some moment, I was valuable and loveable. For lack of a better word."

"You are loveable," Ivy assured her.

"I'm glad you think so, but at that moment, walking up to the door of the house to pick you up, I was so scared, I was ready to throw up." Sophie's lips twisted in a wry smile. "What if you took one look at me and burst into tears? Or screamed?"

"But I didn't."

"No. Your sister Fern did, though," Sophie said gruffly. "You know this story. That blessed child cried for three months straight every time I took her from your father."

"You had to put on his baseball cap and a pair of glasses to get her to calm down." Ivy remembered it. She had almost no memories of Rose being adopted—Ivy had been five and Rose, three at the time—but Fern had arrived as a newborn when Ivy was eleven and Rose was nine, and those memories were brighter. Sharper. "Fern was very loud."

"She's matured nicely." Sophie glanced out the window,

smiling as the antics continued. "You were already fourteen when Tansy joined our family." She gestured to Tansy, who was chasing Dustin Stone as if she were the abominable snowman, arms raised high, mouth open as she roared. "See what changes have occurred in her since that time?"

"Has anything changed?" Ivy asked dryly. "She's still trouble."

Sophie laughed. "But let's go back to that first moment with you and skip ahead slightly. When we opened the door, there you were. Sitting quietly with a bag in your lap, waiting for us."

"You asked me if I was ready to go home." Ivy didn't know if the memory was hers or formed from hearing the story a million times over the years.

Sophie swallowed hard. "That's when I realized it didn't matter how scared I was. It didn't even matter if you loved me, because I had enough love inside me for both of us."

Ivy was sniffling now as well. "I do love you. So much."

"I know," her mother whispered. "Just like you already love Chloe and Harper. Which means if you're not able to be out there running around, well, you'll show them that love in a quieter way. You'll be a soft hand to tend to their hurts. You'll be the place they come for comfort. Someone to share joys and sorrows that don't require fireworks or cannon shots fired."

A gentle peace stilled the aching pulse inside. "Is there a book where I can learn how to give great motherly advice?" she asked. "Because you're really good at it."

Sophie leaned in and kissed her. "One step at a time, my darling. One step at a time."

They hugged. Her mother's love warmed Ivy as much as her embrace did.

Ivy's phone rang. Distracted by the sweet moment with her mom, she considered letting the message go to voice mail. Still, she glanced at the screen.

Her heart leapt into her throat at the number displayed. *Oh my goodness.* She scrambled to answer it. "Hello?"

"Hi, Ivy. Jennifer Tait here. I know this is last minute, but if you're ready, so are we. Everything is signed. I can bring the girls by tonight or tomorrow morning—"

"Tonight," Ivy interrupted, adrenaline flooding her system. "Oh, please, tonight is wonderful."

"See you in an hour, then." Jennifer hung up.

Ivy stared at the phone blankly for a moment before her mother nudged her arm. "Ivy?"

She met her mother's gaze, the wonder of the moment making her voice shake. "They're on their way."

3

———————

As far as distractions went, Walker's extended family knew how to deliver.

Luke and Kelli had teamed up with Caleb's girls, and the four of them lobbed snowballs in random directions, not really caring what they hit. The erratic missiles made it tough to get across the yard unscathed.

Walker ducked behind a tree, nearly stepping on Tucker and Ginny in the process. His sister and her fiancé were busy making snowball after snowball, saving them in a huge pile.

"Don't mind if I do," Walker said, nabbing one off the top of the stack.

"Hey, those are for the final battle," Ginny complained, but she blew him a kiss. "Ivy's waving at you from the porch. Make a break for it—we'll cover you."

Walker peeked from behind the tree, checking how wildly the battle raged between him and his target. "Going...now!"

He rushed into the yard, dodging to the right then rolling. When he popped up, a startled shout exploded in his face. His younger brother stood before him, shocked at Walker's sudden appearance. Dustin teetered, windmilling his arms as he fought for balance.

Too tempting. Walker shifted just enough to nudge his baby brother backward.

"No fair," Dustin cried, a grunt following as snow squeaked under him.

Sudden satisfaction struck. After a quick glance to either side to make sure he wasn't about to be ambushed, Walker closed the distance to where Ivy waited for him on the back porch.

He admired the pretty colour in her cheeks then frowned when he realized she'd pulled on her coat but still wore house slippers and no gloves or toque. "You need to bundle—"

"They're coming. Now. Like, *right* now."

Walker paused, glancing around the yard at all the family. He didn't see anyone missing—

Oh. Oh, *hell*.

He caught Ivy's fingers. "The girls? *Now?*"

She laughed. "You look like I feel. Oh, Walker. They're on their way. They'll be here in under an hour."

He snatched her up and spun her in a circle before kissing her thoroughly. When he finally got himself under control, the noise of the yard had faded to a dull roar.

Caleb met his gaze. "News?"

Walker's heart pounded so hard, he vibrated with it. "They're on the way."

A whoop went up, echoed by a dozen others.

Then Tansy whistled, loud and sharp, catching the entire group's attention as she jumped up on the snow-covered picnic table. "Okay, everybody out of the pool. Follow the plan. We'll all wait patiently for our turn to meet the new sweeties."

Arms swinging as if she were an air traffic controller, Tansy got the mess of them moving. Laughter continued to ring, and all his siblings paused briefly on their way out to pat Walker on the back. Yet like magic, only moments later, the yard was empty.

Bemused, Walker led Ivy back inside the warm house.

She shook her head as she pulled off her coat. "I can't believe they all left like that. *What* plan was Tansy talking about?"

"I'm as lost as you," Walker admitted.

Although, he was glad someone had made a plan. He and Ivy wanted to make the girls' first days in the house quiet and peaceful, and that was not what they would have walked into.

"Tansy and Kelli came up with it," Sophie informed them. Walker peered around Ivy to find his mother-in-law at the front door. She had her boots on already, and Malachi was slipping her coat over her shoulders. "In case we had to get out of the way quickly. Which it appears we do."

Ivy raced across the room to hug her mom while Walker accepted Malachi's handshake.

"You don't have to leave," Ivy told them.

"We're really looking forward to meeting the girls, but this moment is for you," Sophie insisted. She glanced at her husband. "Which means no pulling the car around the corner then sneaking back to peek in the window."

Malachi pressed a hand to his chest. "Would I do such a thing?"

She raised a brow.

He grinned sheepishly. "You know me too well. Come, sweetheart. Let's let the kids have a moment before they meet their family."

Walker's heart did another thump. Their family.

Their *girls*.

The door closed behind his in-laws, and sudden quiet filled his ears.

Ivy slid her hand into his and tugged him toward the living room couch then settled them side by side. She rested her head on his arm, and they sat there for a moment. Stillness took them.

It was deceptive. His brain *raced*. Ivy was probably fighting the same sensation.

"Are you a little scared?" Ivy asked.

"Yes," he admitted freely. "But every time the fear hits, I think of what the girls must feel right now, and it sobers me up hard." He tucked his arm around her, cradled her close, and drew strength from the contact. "It's going to be a challenge at times, and we know that. Hell, my parents dealt with the five of us, six in the summers when Tucker was around. They had to have wanted to pull out their hair at the antics we all got up to."

"My parents had Tansy to deal with," Ivy offered dryly before cuddling in tighter. "Kidding. We were all equally challenging for different reasons, but I know how valuable it all was."

"Exactly. They're kids. They deserve to be loved, period. That, we can give them. The rest?" He kissed her temple. "We'll muddle through."

"Together," Ivy said firmly. She exhaled hard then nodded, her fingers tracing circles on his thigh. "I love you, Walker."

He was so gone. "Love you, Snow."

The quiet was still there, but now it was pulsing with something only definable as hope.

When the front bell rang, he didn't jump out of his skin. He just squeezed Ivy once more then rose and made his way to the door.

Their social worker, Jennifer, stood on the porch, talking quietly with the girls. Harper and Chloe both wore backpacks like Walker's nieces used for school, and they had small rolling suitcases with them.

The sum total of their possessions.

"Hello. We're here," Jennifer said cheerfully.

"Come in." Walker stepped outside. "I'll grab your cases for you."

Jennifer motioned to the door. "Come on, girls."

Chloe moved first. She caught hold of her little sister's fingers. "It's okay, Harper. This is our new house, 'member?"

Harper shrugged, but she walked forward. Her sudden gasp made Walker hurry to see what had happened.

Harper had wiggled out of Chloe's grasp, racing over to stare at Ivy in awe. "You're here."

Ivy smiled, kneeling to unzip Harper's coat and help take off her boots. "This is my home. And now it's yours too."

Walker stood with the suitcases by the door and offered Jennifer his hand. He spoke quietly. "Thank you for bringing them today."

"It worked out best for everyone," she said softly. "The foster home they were in accepted a new family group that arrives tomorrow."

Chloe was stuck with one boot on, so Walker dipped to help. "I like your boots," he told her. "Unicorns are my second favourite animal."

She eyed him.

"Horses are my first," he said. "Remember I told you we have horses at the ranch? And a couple here at the house as well. You'll have to learn how to act around them so you can find out how fun they are too."

Ivy stood. "Jennifer. Would you like some tea? I was going to make some."

The social worker shook her head. "I need to head out. I should let you all get settled." She stooped and met the girls' eyes. "You have a good forever home here. I'll be by in a few days to hear all the wonderful things you have to share."

Chloe caught hold of Harper, and the two of them stood welded together like a statue.

"Goodbye for now. I'll see you soon," Jennifer promised. "Ivy, Walker. Many blessings."

"We've already got them," Walker said.

He closed the door after her and wondered at the sensation. As if he were balancing butterflies on his fingertips. Precious and delicate and so very fragile.

He turned to find three sets of eyes on him.

Time to try this father thing on for size. "Your mommy and I thought you'd like to see your room first. Let's go put your things away," Walker suggested.

He caught hold of their suitcases and carried them down the hall to the biggest of the three bedrooms they'd added.

Behind him, Ivy herded the girls forward. Her quiet voice sounded soft but clear. "For now, we've put you in the same room. If you want your own rooms down the road, we'll rearrange things."

One of the stories Ivy had shared with them was how she and her sister Rose had often ended up tucked into each other's beds in the early years. They might as well expect it.

Walker placed the suitcases on the floor then watched with interest to see their reactions.

Chloe once again held Harper's hand, but now it might be more to keep herself vertical. She stared wide-eyed around the room, taking it all in as if it were magic and might vanish at any moment.

Ivy and her sisters had done a great job preparing a welcoming sight. The quilts on the beds were rainbows, and the pale yellow walls displayed brightly coloured paintings of everyday, ordinary items. Neon-pink shoes. A sunshine-yellow balloon. A pair of puppies in bright-blue top hats.

Chloe smiled as she spotted the last one.

Walker made a note to introduce the girls to the animals at Silver Stone as soon as possible, especially the dogs and kittens.

Also, he needed to keep working on Ivy regarding his idea to get a dog for the family when it was appropriate.

But for now, he did this small, important thing, falling more and more in love the entire time.

Walker sat on the floor beside Harper, opened her suitcase, and listened as she seriously explained to him what each item was and which were her favourites. She lined up the meager collection of clothing in her dresser in neat rows. She prattled about her stuffed moose and found the perfect place for him on her big girl bed.

Then she got distracted and climbed onto Chloe's bed to see what her big sister was doing.

It was a picture Walker wanted to remember forever.

Ivy sat on the bed, resting against the wall. Chloe leaned in as close as she could get without touching. The two of them were immersed in a picture book as Ivy read dramatically. A half dozen other books lay scattered on the mattress beside them.

Chloe's suitcase was still half-full. The bookcase against the far wall had obviously gotten higher billing than unpacking.

Walker pushed the suitcase aside so he could join them. Unpacking could wait. Right now, his family was listening to a story.

4

———

Every morning would be like a new beginning, Ivy thought. Some would be good, some rougher. But every morning was also another day to turn them into a stronger family.

She and Walker had carefully considered how to make the transition as easy as possible on the girls. For their first week together, they had planned simple meals and activities that were calm yet inviting.

Family was to be introduced slowly, but soon, beginning the very first morning with Ivy's eager parents.

"Hello, girls," Sophie said quietly as she settled on the couch, lowering a large handbag to the floor. "I'm your grandma. That means my job is to tell you stories, and give you cuddles, and have lots of fun times together."

Harper moved closer, an adorable frown creasing her forehead. "Gamma?"

Sophie grinned. "Yes. I have other names, but that's a special one for you to use."

"Carter has a grandma," Chloe informed her bluntly. "She doesn't tell stories."

"Well, this gamma does," Sophie returned easily, using Harper's pronunciation.

Her mother's smile shone a little less brightly for a moment, though, and Ivy felt the wave of concern as well. Mention of their brother's situation never seemed to be positive. Chloe and Harper spoke of him often, and obviously cared for him, but something was off.

Ivy and Walker had agreed it was important to keep the sibling visitations going. She had already arranged one for later that week. Hopefully meeting Carter's grandmother in person would put some of their fears to rest.

Sophie leaned forward until she and Chloe were eye to eye. "Would you like to look in the bag? We brought some books with us. Some you might be able to read to me."

As Chloe dug in the bag, Ivy turned her attention to what Walker, Harper, and Malachi had been up to.

She'd seen her dad do all sorts of wild things over the years, so she'd figured he'd get a kick out of having grandkids. But the sight of him playing Barbies on the floor with Harper was priceless.

A moment later it was clear the dolls were all playing roles in a fairy-tale story. "Oh, no. There's a bear walking into the house where Goldilocks is sleeping." Ivy's father had put an exceptionally furry coat over the doll's head to make it more bearlike. "*Grrrrrr*, who's been sitting in my chair?"

"*Grrrrrr*," Harper echoed, an adorable baby bear without even trying. "*Grrrr*, Gampa."

Ivy's parents left just before noon with promises to have the family over for dinner later in the week.

"I'll get the soup going," Walker offered. He turned to Chloe. "Come help me make sandwiches."

"We'll tidy up in here," Ivy said, still cradling Harper after her father had asked for, and been given, a farewell hug. "Right, sweetie?"

Harper pressed her hands to Ivy's face. "Angel lady."

Oh, my. That was one to redirect. "I'm not an angel. I'm your mommy. And we have chores to do before we have lunch with Daddy and Chloe. Can you help? We'll put the toys in the bucket, then we'll put the books from Gamma and Gampa on the shelf."

"I like Gampa," Harper informed her.

"Me too," Ivy said brightly. She scooped up a couple of doll outfits and turned to stuff them into their bag—

She could have sworn there was a face at the window.

"What was that?" Ivy rose and peered outside.

Three faces tilted toward her. Her sisters, bundled up against the cold, crouched under the window.

Ivy shook a finger at them, but amusement slid in as well. "You are not supposed to be here yet," she scolded.

"I know we're early, but we can't wait. Please let us in," Tansy begged.

As if she would send them away. Ivy gestured them forward.

"Be good," she warned before calling to Walker. "We'll need more soup. My sisters are here."

Walker poked his head around the corner as the front door opened, and Tansy, Rose, and Fern poured in. "I figured. Hi, ladies. Wash up. You're just in time for lunch."

Harper had pushed the final book onto the shelf and now stood with her arms wrapped around Ivy's leg, thumb in her mouth.

Ivy picked up her youngest daughter. "Harper, these are my little sisters. They're bigger than your sister, but they're still littler than me. They're going to have lunch with us, so they need to wash their hands. Can you show them where we do that?"

Harper squeezed Ivy's neck tightly, but then she nodded and wiggled to be put down. "My baf-room. I have soap. It makes nice bubbles."

She marched forward, followed by three eager adults who all somehow managed to crowd into the bathroom and still give Harper room as she pulled over and climbed on the short stool she needed to turn on the water.

To Ivy's joy, Harper proceeded to not only wash her hands but supervise and help the handwashing business.

Fern had left her prosthesis off that morning. Harper pointed at Fern's short left forearm. "Ouch."

Fern laughed. "No, not ouch. I was born with a teeny arm. I have nublets instead of fingers, see?" She showed Harper and let her new niece touch. "I have a special robot arm I wear sometimes, but sometimes I take it off."

Harper wiggled her ten fingers and two hands in the air. "Mine stay here."

"Yes," Fern said with amusement. "Yours are very firmly attached. Both types of hands are good, though. And we're all washed up. Are you ready to take me to lunch?"

Harper dried her hands again then carefully caught Fern's fingered right hand. "No fingers on teeny arm."

"Only tiny ones. You can still hold them if you want to," Fern assured Harper as she tugged them down the hall to the kitchen.

Rose slid an arm around Ivy. "She's a delight."

"Both girls are." Ivy rested her head on Rose's shoulder. "Thanks for coming early, even if you crashed Tansy's master schedule."

"Tansy made it, so I figured she could break it," Rose said with a wink. "Come on, I want to meet Chloe as well."

Another moment of perfection followed. A table with her sisters, husband, and daughters all gathered. Tansy, Rose, and Fern stayed in uber-quiet mode but still told stories and shared happy thoughts, and by the end, even Chloe smiled at them a few times.

Lunch flowed into the afternoon. Ivy's sisters left. Naps were taken, more stories read. Nighttime rituals were begun, with family time and cuddles and being tucked into bed.

The fourth morning after the girls arrived, Ivy walked into their room to discover Harper curled up on the floor, her stuffed moose under her head as a pillow. She'd pulled the quilt off the bed. It was easy to discover the reason for the change of location. Harper's bed was wet, and her soggy pajamas had been abandoned on the sheets.

Poor little thing. Ivy went to the floor, stroking the hair off Harper's face. "Hey, sweetie. Did you have an accident?"

Harper whimpered and cuddled tighter against her moose.

An instant later, Chloe was there, pushing herself between Ivy and Harper.

Ivy eased back to give them both room. "It's okay. Accidents happen, and we have a washer and dryer. But let's get you a nice warm bath before you get dressed. Do you want to have a bath with her, Chloe?"

Chloe nodded. She pulled a sleepy Harper to her feet then hauled her toward the bathroom.

It wasn't the first time Ivy had noticed how protective Chloe was of her sister. The behaviour was expected yet another reminder that they were building this family from the base up.

It was going to take time. That was okay.

Ivy took off the sheets and loaded the machine, but even after they were washed, the girls' room still had a funny smell to it.

"I don't understand," she told Walker quietly as they prepared dinner that night. The girls were setting the table, cutlery and dishes clattering. "The beds are fresh, but it's still funky in there."

"If we had two little boys, I'd tell you that was just how they smell, but let me look." Walker slipped away.

He was back in only a few minutes, his face unreadable as he placed a paper bag on the counter beside her.

"What's that?" Other than atrociously smelly.

"Food," Walker said softly. "Sandwiches, mostly. I think from when Chloe helped me at lunch the other day. But I also see half a grilled cheese sandwich from yesterday's lunch and a couple of buns from dinner last night."

Ivy was still confused. "Where was it?"

"In Chloe's bottom dresser drawer."

Oh. Ivy sighed. "She's hiding food. Just in case we stop feeding them?"

Walker pulled her against him and squeezed her tight. "Breathe, love. We'll get them through this. She's still uncertain and determined to protect Harper anyway she can."

"And she's probably been right to hide stuff in the past." Ivy nodded. "We need to talk to her about it."

She stayed there for one more moment, though, drawing strength from Walker. They had a bit of juggling ahead, and she was so glad to have him by her side.

5

___

They waited until after lunch was over. Walker brought out a box of LEGOs for Harper, placing it nearby so Chloe could see her little sister but far enough away that Harper wouldn't overhear.

Ivy took a deep breath then smiled at her oldest daughter. Praying for wisdom like her mother had shown so many times over the years. "Daddy and I want to talk to you about something important."

Chloe held on to her chair, legs kicking wildly. She sank her teeth into her lower lip, worry on her face.

"You and Harper coming to live with us makes us very happy. We *want* to be your mommy and daddy, and that means we promise to always take care of you."

Chloe glanced at Walker then back at Ivy. "Our other mommy isn't happy."

"No. Your birth mommy is sick, but she loves you and wants you to be safe, and healthy, and have lots of good things to eat." Walker said it quietly, but Chloe started squirming. "That's why she agreed we should be your forever mommy and daddy. That is never going to change. You're our forever family now. So you never have to worry about being hungry or cold, or worry that Harper is hungry or cold."

"*Her* place is cold," Chloe whispered.

"You aren't going back to that other house," Ivy said softly. "We'll make sure our house—*your* house—stays nice and warm. And that there's always good things to eat."

"I liked lunch," Chloe said. "Harper did too."

"I'm glad," Ivy said, spying the basket on the counter and getting an idea. "But sometimes, you might get hungry when it isn't time for lunch or supper. Do you know what to do then?"

Chloe shook her head.

"Well, you can ask me or Daddy, and we'll make you a snack." Ivy met Walker's eyes. "Plus, we'll make some special snacks that are ready all the time. When you want one, you can eat it. Does that sound good?"

Disbelief was strong on her face, but Chloe nodded.

"The only rule is snacks get eaten at the table. There's no food allowed in your bedroom or in the play areas. Can you remember that?" Ivy asked.

The little girl stilled.

"We know you're still worried about how things will go, but we do love you and Harper, and we promise to make sure you always have what you need." Walker put the bag of food on the counter, and Chloe wilted.

"We're not mad you hid the food," Ivy said. "But loving you means we want you to be healthy. This food isn't healthy anymore. So let's make some snack bags together, and then you and Harper can eat them when you want. You don't need to hide food, okay?"

Chloe dipped her chin but stayed quiet.

Together they cut up some fruit and tucked it into small plastic containers that fit into the door of the fridge. They poured cereal into snack-sized ziplock bags.

Harper came over to see what was happening just in time to

be propped up on a high stool to help. More Cheerios ended up on the counter than in her bag, but it was a small price to pay to take one more step toward a happier future.

Especially when, after they finished tucking the bags into the basket and the fruit into the fridge, Chloe tentatively told them, "I'm hungry."

She reached into the basket and pulled out a bag, watching Walker and Ivy closely to see their reactions.

Harper reached for a treat as well, ready to open it right then and there.

But Chloe led her to the table. "We have to sit here to eat it."

"'Kay. I like Cheer-os," Harper announced as she crawled up into her booster seat.

"Me too." Walker joined them with his own little stash of cereal. He poured his on the table, and Harper bounced up in her chair, leaning forward to help him. She fed them into his mouth one at a time. He pretended to nibble on her fingers, and Harper snickered and giggled with childish enthusiasm.

Chloe watched with a cautious wisdom beyond her years, holding back her judgment but content for now.

Ivy was still thinking about the situation a couple days later on Saturday, when Chloe and Harper's big brother, Carter, arrived with his grandmother for their sibling visit. The woman lived one small town away to the south, and their social worker had mentioned it might take some time to organize the visit. But when Ivy had called to arrange the playdate, she'd agreed immediately.

Eight-year-old Carter rushed in the door, jerked off his shoes, then tumbled into Chloe and Harper with a rush of excitement. Chloe had him by the hand, pulling him eagerly to the pile of toys she and Harper had brought into the open playroom area off the living room.

Walker greeted the woman politely. "Thanks for bringing Carter over."

"It was fine. I had to come to Heart Falls to pick up a package at the post office anyway. Damn thing was supposed to arrive at Lindsor, but it got sent here instead." She peered around the house, not once glancing at the children. "Nice place."

"Thank you." Ivy gestured into the kitchen area. "I have tea or coffee, whichever you prefer."

"Coffee's good. Cream and sugar." Stephanie settled in the chair beside the cookies and helped herself to one. She pointed toward the back yard. "Quite the spread, but I don't know about your neighbours."

Ivy paused then realized Stephanie was talking about the cemetery on the next property over. "Well, they're definitely nice and quiet."

Stephanie snorted. "I heard you're a teacher."

"Vice principal at Heart Falls Elementary, and grade two teacher. But I'm on leave for the rest of the school year to spend time with the girls."

Ivy placed the coffee in front of the other woman and settled on the opposite side of the table. The position allowed her to speak to Stephanie and still watch the girls and Carter play together.

Carter's hair was lighter than the girls, his facial features a little sharper. His skin tone was a little darker, and he was also thinner than Ivy thought healthy. Still, he smiled and laughed as he pushed a car forward, and Chloe laughed back.

Seeing her face light up was worth everything.

Walker had joined the children, unobtrusively helping put together sections of the racetrack they were building.

"Must be nice to take off time like that," Stephanie commented, bringing Ivy's attention back to her guest. "I'm still punching the clock myself at the grocery store. Always hard to get shifts, especially since I've got to stay home or be back to work around Carter getting to school." She drummed her fingers on the table. "Mind if I smoke?"

"I'm sorry, we don't allow smoking in the house," Ivy said clearly. "But if you'd like, we could go outside."

Stephanie waved a hand. "Guess I can wait." She eyed the children for a bit then turned back. "He's a looker."

Ivy blinked. Oh. She wasn't talking about the children. "Walker? Um, yes."

"What's he do? I couldn't make heads or tails of that message from the social worker."

"Walker owns a ranch with his brothers."

"A farmer, eh?" Stephanie glanced at him again then shook her head. "Too pretty to be a farmer. Too bad you couldn't have your own kids. They'd have been knockouts."

Ivy's brain and mouth seemed to have disconnected from each other. She couldn't for the life of her think of a polite response.

Not that Stephanie seemed to need one. She carried on sipping her coffee and sharing gossip. "Lindsor's not much bigger than Heart Falls, but I think it's a far better place. None of those uppity big-city shops trying to set up. Why, I saw a place near the post office here in Heart Falls that had flowers all over in the windows and some fancy coffee shop right next door. Probably charge ten dollars a cup for bad coffee and day-old cake."

Ivy sipped her tea and resisted telling Stephanie that her sisters owned the place.

"Nope, Lindsor is good enough for me. Good enough for that boy." She tilted her head toward Carter. "I'll probably have to deal with him until he grows up enough to land himself in prison too, just like his daddy."

"We never know how much good we can do in someone's life by being there for them," Ivy offered. "I know at the school, we—"

"My son never listened to me. Don't know why I should expect his son to do anything different," Stephanie interrupted.

Okay, then. These visits were going to be awkward going forward. With nothing in common and Ivy developing a rapidly growing dislike for the other woman.

Ivy tried to be understanding. It had to be hard for someone like Stephanie, in her late sixties and caring for a young boy.

"When did you begin fostering Carter?" Ivy asked. She knew some of the details but was curious what twist Stephanie would put on the situation.

"Six long years," Stephanie replied. "He was two, and his mom got herself pregnant with the older girl there." She pointed at Chloe. "A new boyfriend who didn't want him around. 'Course, my Grant was living at home then, so he helped a little. But not much, and then he ran off and got in trouble, so I've had the boy on my own for years."

"If you ever need us to watch Carter for you, please let us know," Ivy offered. "And if you ever want us to bring the girls over to your place to visit with Carter, we're more than willing."

"They're not mine," Stephanie said bluntly. "They asked me to take the girls, you know, when their mother couldn't manage, but hell if I want two more to raise. Not at my age. Bad enough I've got the one brat underfoot, but at least he's blood. Only reason he's worth anything."

Ivy fought her temper, badly wanting to snap at the older woman. But she didn't want Stephanie to stop the visits, not when Chloe and Harper so clearly loved their brother.

But it was a good thing the children were out of earshot with Walker at the moment. What a horrible thing to say. What a horrible way to think of anyone, let alone a child.

Ivy breathed deep then repeated the most important part. "Well, just remember, if you do need help, we're available."

Then Ivy did something she would never have dreamed of doing with any other visitor. She pushed the TV control at

Stephanie. "I'm going to spend time with the children. Please feel free to entertain yourself."

Stephanie grabbed the remote and clicked on a program.

Ivy was gone before she saw what was playing. She pulled on her coat and joined Walker and the children as they prepared to go play in the backyard.

Walker raised a brow. "Everything okay?"

"Everything but my blood pressure," Ivy muttered. "I'll tell you more later."

The hour Stephanie had agreed to for the visit flew past quicker than any of them wanted. They gathered on the front doorstep, Stephanie finishing the last puffs of her cigarette as she stared over the yard at the cemetery and shaking her head lightly.

"Time to go," she announced. "Thanks for the coffee."

"I'll call to arrange another get-together for the children. We can come your direction if that's easier," Walker offered.

Stephanie shrugged then headed down the sidewalk.

Carter paused then peeked up quickly at Ivy and Walker. "Thanks for the visit and the cookies."

"You're welcome. We'll see you soon, okay?" Walker said quietly.

Chloe and Harper hugged Carter then stood on the porch with Ivy and Walker, waving goodbye over and over.

Carter didn't wave back. He turned and followed his grandmother down the walk and into her car, focusing straight ahead as if they weren't there.

Except, as the car pulled away, he turned and stared at his sisters until the car vanished from sight.

6

———

Buzz. *Buzz, buzzzzzz.*

Walker wasn't sure what time it was, but he was still in bed, cozy and warm. Two weeks had passed since the girls had arrived, and he had to admit he was enjoying the time he'd taken off to be with them.

Silver Stone had arranged things for him to have a full six months of paternity leave—his family continued to give. Having Ivy home as well was making things go so much smoother while Chloe and Harper settled in.

Also, sleeping in was always a treat. Ivy was curled up against him—

Wait. She wasn't only cuddled in tight; she was crowding him off his side of the mattress.

Oh. He pushed upright and peered over her.

Harper lay tucked against Ivy on the other side. Thumb in her mouth, fingers clutching Ivy's braid.

Buzzzzzz.

Right. He'd been woken. Someone was at the door.

Walker hurried out of bed, grabbed a robe, and jerked it on as he strode through the house.

Robes. Huh. He'd never owned one before in his life, but it had seemed the thing to keep from shocking the girls so he could pace the house without getting fully dressed.

He peeked through the side panel of the front door then opened it wide, blinking in surprise. "Ginny? Tucker?"

"Move it, big bro. Things to do, bacon to consume." Ginny pushed past him, an oversized basket hanging off her arm as she called into the house, "Ivy. Wake up. Chloe, Harper. I need your help."

His sister was a force of nature. Walker shook the cobwebs from his brain and turned to Tucker. "Good morning, I guess."

His sister's fiancé grinned. "Morning. Sorry about the wake-up call, but when Ginny gets an idea in her head, there's no stopping her."

"I know," Walker grumbled. He stretched briefly before excusing himself. "Make yourself at home. Ginny obviously has."

Tucker's laughter drifted behind him as Walker returned to his bedroom to get dressed. He paused on the way to check the girls' room. Chloe wiggled in her bed, half-awake, half asleep.

Staring at her for a moment was a necessity.

By the time he closed the door and reached his bedroom, Ivy's eyes were open, and she blinked hard. She glanced at Harper, who was still curled against her, then spoke quietly. "What's up?"

"We are, I guess. My sister has decided to invade. She brought breakfast." He paused. "At least it looks as if she brought breakfast."

"How's that...never mind. It's Ginny. I get it." Ivy curled her arms around Harper and cuddled her closer, happiness making Ivy's face shine. "We'll be up in a little while. This is too sweet to cut short."

"Agreed." Walker leaned in and kissed Harper's forehead.

"Love you, little one." Then he planted one on Ivy. "Love you too."

She winked then closed her eyes and held Harper tight.

Out in the kitchen, Ginny had the promised bacon on the stove reheating, the coffee going, and a pan heating to make pancakes.

"I guess if you plan to wake the entire house, cooking eases the pain," Walker teased his sister.

She plopped a huge mug of coffee in front of him then topped up Tucker's as well.

"What, no sugar?" Tucker complained.

Ginny set the coffee pot on the table then dropped into Tucker's lap to kiss him thoroughly.

"My eyes," Walker complained, but he laughed.

It was good to see his kid sister so obviously in love. And Tucker was the next thing to a brother, so having him around wasn't an issue.

Tucker sighed contentedly as Ginny sprang to her feet. He patted her on the butt before she stepped out of range. "Still need sugar, goddess."

"Softie.

His future brother-in-law's gaze stuck to Ginny's ass like glue. "That's not what you said last night."

"Okay, that's enough," Walker protested. "Some things, I don't need to hear."

"You're so rude," Ginny complained to Tucker, but she laughed too hard to be seriously offended. "On a different topic, Walker, how are things going?"

How to sum up the way his world had changed in a few short weeks?

Impossible, especially with the wild range of emotions he and Ivy had been dealing with. There were challenging moments with Chloe and Harper, but so many more were full of joy.

Harper was still wetting the bed, but only when she slept alone. When she crawled in with Chloe or into bed beside Ivy, she had no problems.

Chloe remained reluctant to smile, but so far they hadn't discovered any more food stashes.

But it was Carter who had returned to Walker's mind over and over. Poor kid. The boy was stuck in a hard place, and all he and Ivy could do was try to make a difference in the small moments they got.

Walker pushed aside his worries and considered all the good things, and suddenly he knew exactly what he needed to share.

He offered his sister an easy smile. "You need kids. Stat."

"I have kids," she said. "Three from Caleb, three from Dare, and now two from you. Plus, there always seems to be someone visiting Silver Stone who brings a baby or two to cuddle."

Walker shook his head. "If you didn't love kids, or didn't eventually want ones of your own, I wouldn't say this. But you're a kid person, Ginny. And I'm telling you, there's no explaining what it feels like when they're your own. It's so much more. I love Caleb's kids, but Harper and Chloe have their fingers around my heart."

"Sounds dangerous," Ginny returned, hugging him tight. "I'm so happy for you. You and Ivy both."

"Thanks."

She whirled off to the stove and proceeded to clatter and bang to her heart's content.

"I'm serious. Work on the kid thing," Walker suggested, meeting Tucker's gaze. The man deserved a little harassment for his earlier comment. "Ask if you need advice on how to make that happen."

"Let me get the other item off the checklist first," Tucker told him.

"Which is?"

Tucker chin-lifted toward Ginny. "She'll tell you soon enough. It's why we're here."

"Fine. I'll hold my questions. What's up at Silver Stone?" Walker finished waking up as Tucker shared the latest news from the ranch.

Chloe and Harper made it to the kitchen in their pyjamas. Harper came over and hugged Walker then lifted her head for him to give her a kiss.

Chloe still hung back. She smiled, though, then examined Tucker, her glare lightening when she recognized him.

"Hey, kiddo," Tucker said. "Steal a piece of bacon for me?"

Walker frowned. "*Tucker.*"

The other man's eyes opened wide, then he coughed. He'd been told about the food stashing incident but had obviously forgotten. "Right. Sorry. May I *please* have a piece of bacon, Auntie Ginny?"

She grabbed one off the platter and brought it to him. "Love you," she murmured as she kissed his temple. "Trouble."

"Love you too. Thanks for my bacon," he called after her. Then he asked Harper, "Want half?"

Harper shook her head, leaning harder against Walker.

He didn't mind. Not one bit.

"It smells wonderful in here." Ivy paused beside the kitchen island. "Thanks for coming over, Ginny."

"You're welcome." She grabbed a cup and pressed it into Ivy's hands. "Now that we're all here, to the living room," she ordered.

Ivy met Walker's gaze.

He shrugged. "Your guess is as good as mine at this point, but she did bring bacon and has pancake stacks started. I vote we let her roll with it."

Ginny stuck out her tongue at him then darted ahead into the comfortable living room.

She directed everyone to where she wanted them to sit. The

girls on one couch; her, Walker, and Tucker on the other. Ivy was left to her own devices.

Then Ginny leaned forward on her elbows and spoke to the girls.

"Uncle Tucker and I are getting married in a couple of weeks," Ginny reminded them. "That's what this means." She held up her hand with the shiny ring on it.

Harper crawled onto the couch, staring across the distance at Ginny's ring. "It's purdy."

"It is. So, when we get married, it's a tradition to have other pretty things around," Ginny said.

"Around the *bride*," Tucker slipped in quickly. He straightened and patted his chest proudly. "The groom gets to be handsome and smart and totally awesome. That's my job."

Chloe and Harper both stared at him silently.

He grunted then winked at Walker. "Tough crowd."

Ginny rolled her eyes. "Ignore him. He picked the menu for the wedding dinner. I get to decide the rest."

"Sounds like a great plan." Walker nodded sagely. "The food is the most important part of the day—*ouch*." He rubbed his side where Ginny had jabbed her elbow. "I'm sure that was an accident, Auntie Ginny. We don't poke people in this house."

"Poking brothers is a necessity, so it can't be against the rules." She planted her fists on her hips. "Do you mind? I'm trying to tell the girls something important."

Laughter drifted from the oversized chair Ivy had long ago claimed as her own. "Then tell them," she ordered quietly. "You've got me curious."

Ginny slid onto her knees in front of Chloe and Harper. "When Uncle Tucker and I get married, I have to walk up to where he's waiting, and I get to have people with me to make the trip really special. I want to have all my niblings with me. Sasha and Emma are my maids of honour. Little Tyler will be the ring bearer. And I'd like you two to be my flower girls."

An image flashed into Walker's mind. What it would look like to have his girls as a part of the celebration. He had to turn his face away for a moment to keep it together.

Leave it to Ginny to find a way to make *her* special day about building family connections. About making the girls feel a part of the celebration instead of focusing on only herself and Tucker.

Chloe tilted her head. "I've seen weddings on TV. Will we have fancy clothes? And carry baskets?"

Ginny considered. "Well, the baskets are a yes. The clothes will be nice and new, but we're not doing things too fancy-dancy. We're holding the wedding at Silver Stone in one of the barns, so you'll have to dress up in your best Western clothes."

"Married wif the horses?" Harper whispered in awe.

A soft laugh escaped Ginny. "The horses aren't coming to the ceremony. It's going to be up in the hayloft, and they can't climb stairs."

Chloe slid off her chair and crowded closer. "I want to be a flower girl."

Harper all but crawled into Ginny's lap. "Me too. Wif the kittens."

Because the hayloft was where the kittens lived. Walker was proud as anything at how smart she was to know that already.

"I'm very glad. Thank you." Ginny's expression bloomed with pleasure as she glanced across the room at Walker. She snuck a quick hug with Harper before nodding happily. "Now, let's finish making breakfast. After, we'll look at some pictures online and you can pick your flower girl outfits."

Harper and Chloe skipped off to the kitchen, Tucker going with them.

Ivy paused as Ginny got to her feet. "You're an awesome auntie. Thank you."

"I adore them," Ginny said with a shrug. She caught Walker's eye. "By the way, your tuxedo fitting is on Wednesday. I need my brothers sharp for pictures."

Walker laughed then pulled her in for a hug. "Number one, bullshit on the tuxedo fitting. As if you want us in those monkey suits. And number two, love you." He kissed her cheek. "You're an awesome sister."

Ginny patted him on the back. "Being awesome runs in the family. Now let's go eat bacon."

7

———

INTERLUDE: A WEDDING

GINNY

February 10, Silver Stone ranch

A day of sadness. A day for happiness.

Ginny Stone pulled the brush through her hair slowly, staring out the window at the snowy ground as she finished getting ready.

Memories crowded in.

Fifteen years ago, the Stone family had just found out their parents were never coming home. Rough times followed, emotional times, but eventually, they'd all found ways to live again. To laugh, to pull together, and seek out happiness.

The sadness never really left, but life had moved on and grown sweet again. Which was why Ginny and Tucker had picked this date to get married. Another good memory to layer over the sad ones.

With a mix of emotions tangled around her, she wasn't sure if she was standing on her feet or hovering inches off the ground. Ginny checked the mirror once more, but she was as ready as she was going to get.

She had chosen to wear her long hair down, one side tucked behind her ear as usual. Very basic makeup, mostly some eyeliner and lip gloss for a bit of pop. She looked more than presentable, she figured.

It was time to make sure the newest little Stones had found *their* feet.

Ginny exited the bathroom in her and Tucker's cottage and stepped into the kitchen/living room area. That morning, Ginny's foster sister and best friend, Dare, had returned to Silver Stone with her three boys and husband to help with the final wedding preparations. The small living space in what had originally been Dare's home had been turned into a dressing room and all-around prep room for the women of the wedding party.

Thankfully, it was a small gathering. The four nieces, Ivy, Dare, and herself.

Four-year-old Harper sat on Ivy's lap at the table, more interested in staring at Dare than putting together her flower basket. Chloe had started slowly but was now eagerly poking through all the blooms her new Auntie Rose had brought in a huge bucket from the flower shop.

Dare was helping, mostly by putting rejected stems back into the bucket. She glanced up as Ginny entered the room and winked, but she stayed quiet because Harper was singing tunelessly as she watched her sister. A sweet little-girl song about how flowers loved to dance.

Chloe selected some, rejected others, rearranging hers and Harper's baskets over and over again. By now, some of the stems were broken, and a few petals had fallen off from being handled by little fingers, but to Ginny, the arrangements looked beautiful.

"You have them the way you like them yet?" she asked.

"Almost." Chloe wrinkled her nose and considered. "Needs more blue."

Ginny's oldest niece, Sasha, leaned in from across the table and checked out the baskets with all the wisdom and experience of her thirteen years. "If you add some white flowers, the others will look brighter, including the blue."

The younger girl considered then grabbed another fistful of flowers. She shoved them at Sasha. "Help."

"Sure," Sasha said eagerly.

The sight of them with their heads bent over the baskets was adorable. Ginny met Ivy's gaze, and they smiled at each other.

"Auntie Ginny, this isn't working," Emma complained. "Help it lie straight, please."

Her niece number two had turned down the idea of a jean skirt, a plaid dress, or any of the other options presented to her. She'd seen what Caleb was going to wear and decided if it was good enough for her dad, it was good enough for her. At eleven years old, the black vest over a white shirt paired with a thin leather tie was a sharp contrast to her head full of bouncy blonde curls, but it was what Emma wanted. Which meant Ginny was determined to make it work.

"I can fix this problem. Your shirt needs to be tucked in so the vest doesn't ride up in the back," Ginny instructed as she helped smooth the fabric. "But ask Auntie Ivy to help you with the tie. I'm no good with them."

"Then who helps with Uncle Tucker's ties?" Emma asked seriously.

Ginny couldn't stop her snicker. "Sweetie, I've seen Tucker in a suit exactly never. I don't expect that to change going forward, so if the man needs help, he'll have to come to see your daddy."

"Dad is good at tying ties, but our mom is even better,"

Sasha said easily. She nodded knowingly at Chloe. "Auntie Kelli says ties are like reins on a good horse—"

"Is this Kelli-ism approved for little ears?" Ginny interrupted quickly, because sometimes they turned out to be awfully risqué, no fault of poor Kelli.

Sasha looked confused as she considered. "She says reins and ties are more for show than anything."

Dare laughed. "A very good Kelli-ism."

Ivy motioned Emma forward. "Come, and I'll help fix you. Harper, do you have any flowers you want to add to your basket? We need to go soon, so help Chloe put in the last flowers."

Harper crawled out of Ivy's lap and onto the chair with Chloe to examine her basket. "It's purdy."

"It's very pretty," Sasha agreed. "Do you want to add any more?"

While Harper considered and Ivy finished looping Emma together, Ginny fit herself into her new boots.

"You look amazing. Tucker is going to fall over when he sees you," Dare informed her quietly as she worked. "You look happy."

"I am, and I'm so blessed." Ginny paused before slipping the second boot on then impulsively hugging Dare. "Thanks for coming out on a Thursday to join us."

"Of course." Dare grinned. "Totally not suffering. Since we're sticking around, I get a mini vacation taking care of the old place while you and Tucker go off on your honeymoon."

"*Vacation*? You have Jesse and the three boys with you."

"Ha!" Dare grinned wider. "Between Tamara, Sasha, and Emma, do you really think I'll see hide or hair of my babies the entire time I'm at Silver Stone?"

"Fine. Vacation away. Just no having sex in our bed," Ginny warned in a low whisper.

Dare raised a brow. Snorted.

"Well, fine. At least don't *tell* me about it." Ginny laughed as Dare bumped her in the shoulder.

"I love you, Truth," Dare said with the ease of forever. "I'm so happy for you."

"I love you, Dare," Ginny returned, sneaking in another hug to stop herself from crying before she returned to her task of dressing.

Like the girls, her wedding outfit was simple and bought more for the fact she'd be able to wear the brand-new jeans and pretty cream-coloured blouse more than once. But the cowboy boots were sheer luxury. Top of the line, embroidered to within an inch of their lives, Ginny thought they were the prettiest thing she'd ever seen.

Until she turned and got a peek of all four girls lined up and waiting for inspection.

"We're ready," Emma announced.

In jeans or jean skirts with plaid shirts, three brown-haired girls and one blonde smiled her way. Cute as anything, but it was how they looked together that made Ginny go misty-eyed. She had *four* nieces now, and it felt so right. "You're all beautiful. Pictures before we head over."

She pulled out her phone and snapped a couple.

"Get in there with them," Ivy ordered as she and Dare took out their phones as well. "I want some shots with the bride and her wedding attendants."

Ginny went willingly, somewhat pleased to notice she wasn't the only one wiping her eyes.

"Oops, and one last thing." Dare pulled two chains with rings on them from her pocket. "Harper. Chloe. Your littlest cousin, Tyler, has the sniffles, which means he's a little too germy to help today. He's going to hang out with Auntie Tamara instead of being our ring bearer. That means you two have to hold the rings until Mr. Fields says he needs them. I turned them into necklaces for you to wear."

With awe on their faces, the little girls dipped their heads to accept the chains.

A flurry of potty breaks followed, then coats were pulled over clothes, and they marched from the teeny cottage to the upper level of the main barn for the ceremony.

More of the family waited to help with the final organizing. Dare went to rescue her husband. The girls were whisked away, and Ginny tucked herself into the shadows as she waited.

Before she went with the girls, Ivy gave Ginny a hug, holding on a little longer than typical. "Thank you for those memories," she whispered. "For making this a day they'll never forget."

"Thanks for opening your heart to them," Ginny said. "You're making me think it might be time to get started on a couple kids as well. Although I don't think I'll do the *add two at once* method."

Ivy kissed her cheek then slipped quietly away after her girls.

Ginny stood at the back of the long opening between the hay bales and waited, closing her eyes and picturing her mom and dad. She tried to imagine what they'd say and do in this moment, but the images were blurry. She had good memories of them, had been guided by the wisdom they'd left behind.

But they weren't here now.

"You ready?" Big brother Caleb stood beside her.

Her parents weren't here, but *he* was. Just like he'd always been. Just like all the boys, but Caleb especially had become like a father to her.

Ginny threw her arms around his neck and squeezed tight. "Thanks for being there for me."

"Always," he promised, the word gruff as always but so sweet.

She heard shuffling on her other side and turned. Dustin appeared. His cheeks were flushed red, but he accepted her hug as well. When she'd asked him to walk her down the aisle along with Caleb, her little brother had beamed with pride.

Ginny tucked her hands into the crooks of their elbows, settling them on either side of her as they waited for the girls to go first. "My biggest brother and my littlest brother escorting me down the aisle. Perfect."

Dustin grinned. "Let's get you hitched before Tucker comes to his senses."

Ginny laughed. She glanced toward the far side of the hayloft, where familiar faces of family and friends shone back at her. Malachi Fields waited at the front to oversee the ceremony. Dare stood to one side, her husband Jesse's arm around her shoulders. Their three little boys were arranged in front of them like dominos in a row.

Tamara was at the far edge of the gathering, a sleepy, pink-cheeked Tyler in her arms. His eyelids drooped even as he fought to stay awake. Kelli was there as well, and flashed a quick thumbs up at Ginny.

Luke and Walker—her brothers who'd been her partners in crime most often over the years—grinned her direction from the front. Although Walker could be forgiven if his gaze drifted to his daughters.

Ginny took that all in before meeting Tucker's gaze. He stood between Luke and Walker, tall and solid and so handsome, her heart leapt. He also wore brand-new jeans in a pristine black. He'd covered his white shirt with a black tailored jacket and wore a narrow tie—perfectly knotted—along with a brand-new black cowboy hat.

She knew the girls were walking forward, knew that music played. Her brothers stood on either side of her like tall, strong support pillars. But the love in Tucker's eyes was the biggest and most important thing of all.

When it was finally the right moment, Ginny Stone took a deep breath and walked toward love.

8

INTERLUDE: A WEDDING

TUCKER

The flowers in Harper's basket were wiggling.

Tucker wasn't sure when he first noticed. Between nerves from waiting for the damn ceremony to start, and his excitement of this day finally arriving, there was so much else to deal with.

Walker and Ivy's little girls stood just beyond the spectators seated on the hay bales arranged in two rows. While it could be that Harper was shaking the basket in her excitement, that wouldn't explain the way the flowers *lifted* every now and then.

"You're twitching as if you plan to make a dash for it." Luke eyed him hard. "Don't even think about it."

"If he runs, we'll duct tape him to a horse to bring him back," Walker suggested. "That knocks the fight out of them eventually."

"Comedians, both of you," Tucker said dryly. "I hope someone is keeping an eye on your sister. I figure she's the one who might bolt if she gets the chance."

"Nah. You've somehow got her convinced you're the catch of the century." Luke punched him lightly in the arm. "Good job.

It's going to be so much better to torment you when you're officially a brother."

"Easier? How can it get *easier*? You torment me all the time."

"Look sharp. Movement at the other end of the loft," Walker warned before sighing happily as the music started. Chloe took Harper by the hand, and they started a slow walk toward him. "Aren't they the sweetest damn things? Every time I look at them, my heart goes into overdrive, and I can't stop grinning."

"You're a lucky man," Luke said quietly.

The flower girls were followed by Sasha and Emma, who swayed slowly down the aisle.

But Tucker had spotted Ginny, and he couldn't look away.

Deep-blue jeans contrasted with the cream of her shirt. The shirt was covered in ruffles, and he couldn't wait to dig under the mass to unwrap her once the pomp and ceremony were done. Her dark hair swung around her shoulders, feet firmly marching toward him in cream-coloured boots. Totally impractical, although very pretty, and he grinned.

Ginny being impractical for their wedding day? He was over the moon. Damn woman spent more time thinking about how to make everyone around her happy, so he was glad to see one frivolous thing that meant she was also willing to make herself happy.

A few flowers spilled onto the walkway, catching his attention. Harper hauled her basket higher and braced an arm under it as if the entire thing weighed significantly more than a handful of flowers should.

When a kitten's head poked up briefly, Tucker let his grin free. He caught Ginny's gaze again. The Stone family was always good for a surprise or two. Just because he and Ginny were getting married was no reason for that to change.

He got lost in her eyes again for a bit, because the next thing he knew, girls, flowers, and kitten were all out of sight and Ginny was there. Right in front of him.

She quickly kissed both Caleb's and Dustin's cheeks before pushing them not so gently toward the side. "Out of the way, guys. I'm getting married."

Tucker laughed. "Hey, goddess. You ready for this?"

"Very ready," she assured him. "Hi, Mr. Fields."

"Ginny." Malachi dipped his head. "If you're prepared, I'll get their attention and we can get this done."

"I'm ready," Tucker announced firmly. "Have been forever."

It was Ginny's turn to laugh. "I know. I was so mean to make you wait." She lowered her voice to a sultry tone. "I promise I'll make it worth your while later."

Malachi coughed lightly then raised his voice to the gathering. "And it appears we're good to go."

"Before Ginny says something else that makes you blush," Tucker teased.

The older man shook his head, but he smiled as he began, turning to the gathering. "It's my privilege to be able to preside over events like today. It's always exciting to see two young people want to make a commitment to each other, and to forever. But I'm always reminded that while this is a special event, it's only *one* day. It's a step in a journey it takes years to conclude.

"That's why sometimes when I have a couple share their vows, I feel a little trepidation. I wonder if they know the journey won't always be easy. That the hills will be tiring, and the valleys might be deep, but that even in the hard times, there can be joy." He twisted so he could lay his hands on Tucker's and Ginny's shoulders. "But today I feel nothing but happiness. Not because there's any guarantee your journey forward will be all smooth sailing, but because you've already proven you know how to weather the storms. Together. With each other, and with the support of the people you love and who love you."

Malachi turned them toward the hayloft. Toward the family and friends who sat watching. All the Stones were present, and the Fields family as well. Some of the ranch hands Tucker had gotten to know well over the past year were there, including Alex and his fiancée, Yvette.

Standing at the front and to the left of them was Tucker's uncle Ashton. Contentment radiated from the man as Sonora stood beside him, arm linked through his.

It was exactly as Malachi had said. A collection of people who loved him and Ginny. Whom Tucker loved.

"I'll turn the floor over to you," Malachi said. "Ginny, if you'd like to go first?"

Tucker took her hands as they faced each other. Being there in the hayloft, bales stacked around them in a way so reminiscent of their Operation Prove It headquarters, it felt as if he were coming home.

Ginny squeezed his fingers. "You've been a part of Silver Stone for so long, I barely remember a time without you. And considering the crush I had on you as a teenager, I have to confess I don't really remember a time when I didn't love you. But when I look back, I can see that isn't all of it. The past was beautiful, along with uncomfortable and infuriating," she said wryly. A ripple of laughter spread through the watchers. "These past two years have also been beautiful and uncomfortable, and at times infuriating, but they've been richer. They've been full of time with the real you, without barriers between us, and with real, solid love on the table."

She swallowed hard, her eyes shimmering bright.

Tucker slid a fallen strand of hair behind her ear then cupped her cheek.

She straightened, always so strong. Always so willing to let him see into her very heart. "I love you, Tucker. I'm very glad to walk that long road with you. Through the valleys, or up onto the hilltops where we can linger in the sunshine. But wherever we are, we'll love each other."

Screw it. Tucker leaned forward, right then and there, and

kissed her. Sliding his hand back to cradle her head until the angle was perfect to press their lips together more firmly.

He put everything he felt into the motion.

It was the laughter that finally brought him back.

Ginny gasped for air when he pulled away, but her smile was dazzling. "Man of few words?"

"Oh, I've got plenty of words," Tucker said. "But they boil down to this. I love you. I can't say the same thing as you about having had a wild crush years ago, because that would've been just wrong, all things considered. But I'm a man smart enough to learn when he's taught a lesson. You helped me see pretty clearly that we were meant to be. And if we're talking about journeys, you and Malachi are right. We've already traveled a fair distance down the road together. Today just makes it a little more official. Gives me a chance to say in front of all these people that you mean everything to me and that I plan to spend the rest of my life making sure you know it."

Ginny tilted her head slightly. "Aww, that was sweet."

"I love you," he repeated.

She threw her arms around him and kissed him, and laughter spilled again.

Malachi's slow chuckle rose from close by. "Well, it appears we've already gotten to the celebrating part, but perhaps we should finish the formalities. Are there any rings to be had?"

Sasha patted Chloe on the shoulder, gesturing toward the front.

Harper shuffled forward as well, her eyes wide at all the people smiling at her and her sister.

Ginny knelt to accept the basket from Harper. She peeked in then made a small sound of surprise. "Oh."

Tucker remembered his earlier discovery in time to catch the kitten that sprang from Harper's basket. "Hey, look at this," he said quietly to the little girl. "Another wedding guest?"

"She's helping wif the wing," Harper said seriously. "See?"

A bit of twine was tied around the kitten's belly. Attached to it was the necklace holding the wedding band he'd bought for Ginny.

Tucker could only imagine what would have happened if the cat had decided to escape before this point in the ceremony.

"Wow. Good thing kitty is here so I can use the ring to marry Ginny." He carefully undid the knot, sliding the string, necklace, and ring off the furry creature before carefully placing the kitten in the basket and returning it to Harper. "Thank you."

Chloe lifted the second chain over her head and solemnly handed it and the ring to Ginny. "I only found one string, so I let Harper have it."

Ginny looked ready to burst into laughter, but Tucker managed to nod seriously. "That was very kind of you. Thank you for taking good care of the rings."

The two little girls stood there, baskets in hand, as if waiting for the next part of the show.

Didn't seem any reason to disappoint them. Tucker stayed on one knee where he was so the littlest nieces had a prime view. He caught Ginny as she rose, tugging her to a seat on his horizontal thigh. "Will my bride do me the honour of branding me, so to speak?"

Ginny laughed, winking at Chloe. "The rings are a way of saying love goes on forever. 'Round and 'round, just like the band. See?" She held it up and circled her finger a few times. Then she met Tucker's gaze, and this part was all for him. "And forever is how long I'm going to love you, Tucker. I promise."

She slid the ring on his finger, and peace slid into his soul.

He didn't have any fancy words left in him. He just took the ring he had for her, placed it on her finger, and then kissed her knuckles. "Love you, Ginny. So much."

She caught him by the shoulders and held on tight.

The way he wanted her to hold on to him.

Yup, forever.

9

Early June, Monday morning

Walker was dreaming.

He knew it wasn't real because the scenes kept jumping from place to place. He was in the barns at Silver Stone, pulling chores next to his brothers. Racing down the field at school, trying to catch up with Ivy. For a few moments, he was tucked beside Heart Falls on a summer day, a picnic blanket spread at the edge of the trees and Ivy looking up at him with flushed cheeks.

A swirl of memory later and he was going over the waterfall, limbs flailing as he fell. Before he could hit the lake's surface, he was on the back of a bull, bouncing hard but refusing to give up.

When the buzzer sounded, everything went absolutely quiet, and he was outside in his backyard, leaning on the railing that surrounded their small arena and horse stable.

The girls' playhouse sat a few meters away, a soft light glowing in the open window.

"Walker."

The push on his shoulder was hard enough to break through his dream.

He twisted in the bed to find Ivy eyeing him. The light peeking in the window announced it was nearly time to get up. "Morning."

She snorted. "You were riding a bull, weren't you?"

"Amongst other things." He examined her quickly. "I didn't hurt you, did I? Swinging my arm or something?"

"No, you were fine," she assured him. "Just muttering under your breath a lot. And the eight-second countdown was a bit of a giveaway."

He pulled her against him. "Sorry I woke you."

She slid closer. Soft fingers drifted over his chest. "Well, we're both awake now. We might need to find something to do to pass the time."

"Mrs. Stone, are you trying to seduce me?"

Ivy waggled her brows. "Has it been so long, you can't tell?"

The door to their bedroom squeaked as it inched open. Wordlessly, Harper made her way across the floor to Walker's side of the bed. He turned to lie on his back, and one set of serious brown eyes met his as she tugged softly on the quilt.

After months of being a family, they'd settled into some sweet routines. The girls were happy. Ivy glowed as she enjoyed learning the ropes of motherhood. And impulsive, unplanned sex had become a very rare thing for Walker and Ivy.

He would have to mention to Caleb that he was now fully aware of how tough it was to find time for privacy when there were kids around. His brother would get a kick out of the confession.

"Good morning, Harper. Do you need something?" Walker

asked quietly. Usually she simply crawled into bed on Ivy's side and they discovered her in the morning.

Harper wrinkled her nose a few times then opened and shut her mouth before jerking on the quilt again. "Daddy."

A change that made his heart ache with pride. Harper now called them *Mommy* and *Daddy* easily. Chloe had on occasion, but they'd get there.

"Yes?"

"Daddy help." She tugged again. "Chloe's scared, but Daddy can help."

"Chloe's scared? Show me," he said, tossing back the covers and shoving his feet into slippers. He grabbed his sweatshirt from the previous day and jerked it over his head, following Harper out of the room. A nightmare? It seemed an odd time for it, and so far Chloe hadn't had any issues in that direction.

Harper passed her bedroom and headed forward in a hurry. Walker stuck his head into the room anyway, just for a second, but the two beds were empty. The closet doors were open, and clothes were scattered on the floor.

Ivy was behind him now. "What's wrong?"

"Don't know yet." Walker raced down the hall and into the kitchen. "Harper, where's Chloe?"

The kitchen held more mysteries and no answers. The table was covered with a dozen empty snack bags and fruit containers.

"Shit," Walker murmured. What was going on?

Harper caught him by the hand. "Daddy can help. I tell Chloe, but she's scared."

"Daddy will help," Walker promised. "Where's your sister?"

His youngest daughter pointed outside at the playhouse.

The morning was cool, not cold. Walker ignored his shoes and jacket and ran outside in his slippers.

Nothing could have prepared him for what he found when he opened the door of the playhouse.

Chloe was there—thank God—but so was her brother, Carter. The two of them were curled up like stray kittens, wrapped in the soft throw Ivy used in her living room chair.

Carter's face was streaked with dirt and tear marks. No visible signs of any injuries, but also no clues to the question of how he was here at the house in the first place.

Stephanie had been convinced to bring him for visits once a month. Ivy and Walker paid her gas money then fed her and Carter while she visited. And every other week, Walker had been driving out to pick Carter up for a full day visit on Saturdays. Spending time with the boy and witnessing how happy he was to play with Chloe and Harper had made returning him at the end of each visit harder and harder.

They'd had a visit just two days earlier, and Stephanie had been very thankful for the day off from watching him.

Seeing the little guy in their backyard was a shock.

"Carter. Chloe. What are you doing?" Walker spoke loud enough to wake them but ensured his tone remained gentle.

He had thought the time spent on the drives together had made the boy trust him a little, but when Carter woke up and spotted him, the unexpected happened.

The little guy shot across the playhouse and threw himself at Walker. "I don't want to go away."

Pain drilled into Walker. Here and now wasn't the place to discuss the problems of fostering and family rights. "Come inside the house. Chloe, wake up, sweetie. We need to go see Mommy. And Harper. She wants to know you're safe."

Chloe blinked as she eyed Carter, who clung to Walker like a leech.

She met Walker's eyes. "He ate his snacks at the table," she said clearly. As if proud they hadn't broken any rules.

"Good girl. Now come. We'll have breakfast if you're still hungry."

Chloe took his hand. Walker slowly made his way back to

the house with his daughter at his side and her brother in his arms.

Carter sniffled hugely every now and then, but he didn't cry, and he didn't let go.

Ivy held the door open and let them in without asking any questions. She just took Chloe and held her tightly.

"I'm cold, Mommy," Chloe said quietly. "And Carter's scared."

Walker settled in a chair, keeping Carter in his arms. "We're here now. You don't have to be scared."

Harper patted her brother's back gently. "Daddy will help. He promises."

Carter shook his head, still buried against Walker's neck.

God. So many questions.

Walker met Ivy's gaze over Carter's shoulder. "Take Chloe for a bath to warm up, and call Jennifer?"

"Yes." Ivy stood and took Chloe by the hand. "You come with us, Harper."

The girls left the room. Walker hugged Carter tight. "Okay, bud. Man-to-man talk time. How did you get here?"

"Walked."

Jesus. Walker lifted Carter's chin and looked him in the eye. "All the way from your grandma's apartment to here? That's a good four hours for me."

Carter's face screwed up at the mention of his grandmother. "She's dead."

"*What?*" Walker blinked.

The eight-year-old sniffled then fought tears. "Grandma wouldn't wake up. I don't want a new foster family." He fought for control, barely getting out the rest of the words. "If I move, I won't see Chloe and Harper anymore. Chloe said I could live in the playhouse until I'm a grown-up."

Walker couldn't have stopped the motion if he'd tried. He wrapped his arms around Carter and hugged him tight. He quickly ran through the math in his head. Grandma not waking up? Had to be yesterday morning, which meant Carter had been on his own for nearly twenty-four hours.

How had no one seen an eight-year-old wandering along the side of the highway? For that matter, how had Carter known how to get from one town to the other?

"For now, you'll stay here. We need to talk to some people, and we need to see what's up with your grandma."

"She's dead." This time Carter said it with equal conviction and down-to-earth resignation.

Walker pushed aside that issue for now. "Are you still hungry? Food first, then you get a bath and I'll find you some clean clothes."

The little guy scrambled off Walker's lap, wiping at his eyes. "I'm hungry."

By the time Ivy returned with Chloe and Harper, Carter was halfway through a grilled cheese sandwich and a glass of milk.

The girls climbed into their chairs and eagerly took the plates Walker offered them.

Harper nodded at her brother and sister. "Daddy is a good helper," she informed them before taking a huge bite of her sandwich.

Ivy slid in beside Walker at the stove. "I got a hold of Jennifer. She's going to try to contact Stephanie. What did he say?"

"He thinks Stephanie's dead. He got scared and decided to walk to our house, if you can imagine that."

Ivy's eyes widened. "Oh my God."

"Right? To all of it."

She glanced at Carter. "Okay, until we know more, we'll feed him and wash him up. See if we can convince him to take a nap. Chloe said he woke her by tapping on their window. She let him in the house and fed him, but he didn't want to stay inside."

"Poor kid," Walker said softly, watching the siblings as they chatted quietly. Harper was the only one who was light and happy. Carter was understandably subdued compared his usual self. Chloe still looked worried, clearly understanding this wasn't a normal visit.

"They're quiet when they want to be," Ivy said with concern. "I had no idea anyone was in the house."

"Time to get a dog," Walker suggested slyly.

"*Walker*." Ivy gave him the look. The one that said if he mentioned getting a dog around the girls, she would skin him.

"Just saying, a good dog would have let us know Carter was around."

Okay, so it wasn't time yet. But getting a dog *was* on the list—and the ones on the ranch weren't here at their house.

The children ate their fill of grilled cheese, then Ivy got the girls started on their usual chores while Walker escorted Carter to the bathroom. He was desperately trying to remember what age his brother had mentioned the nieces did this unsupervised.

Screw it. The kid needed to be clean, and Carter needed to know he had adults around who cared.

"Soap there, and shampoo. We'll use both," Walker said firmly, remembering that when he was a kid, bathing involved jumping under the water then getting out as fast as possible.

While Walker got the water going, Carter stripped off his muddy clothes. He got in the tub, a too-skinny little boy with mud on his face and sadness in his eyes.

Walker helped, pouring out shampoo. Getting a washcloth full of soap and making sure it got used. By the time Carter was clean and in a borrowed outfit made of bits and pieces they'd found, the boy smelled better, and his eyelids were drooping.

He found a spot as close to Walker as possible on the couch and curled up against him while they waited for news.

Harper came and offered a hug. "Don't be sad, Carter. Daddy helped, and Mommy. They'll love you."

It was far too true. Walker met Ivy's gaze as the phone rang.

He wondered if it was possible to stop falling even more in love with the boy when Walker felt to the core of his being that Carter belonged in their family as well.

10

—————

Ivy rose as she answered the phone, slipping into the quiet of the kitchen. "Jennifer?"

"Yeah, hi. I have news for you and Walker. How's Carter?"

"He's okay. We've fed him, and he's had a shower, and he's about to fall asleep on the couch. How is Stephanie?"

"She's alive. But can I talk with you and Walker without the kids hearing, please? That will save me explaining this twice."

"Just a minute." Ivy peeked into the living room. Carter had curled up with his head on Walker's lap. His sisters had both pulled books from the shelf and were reading quietly, although Chloe was mostly staring at her brother.

Walker's gaze was fixed on Ivy, and when she motioned him over, he eased out from under Carter. "Girls, stay here with your brother. Mommy and I need to talk."

Chloe's gaze drifted after him as he joined Ivy in the kitchen.

"Jennifer. She wants to talk to us," Ivy shared quickly. "Stephanie is alive."

"God, Carter will be glad." But Walker's expression tightened and so did the band of fear around Ivy's heart.

She'd begun to hope they could keep him, which was a terrible confession, considering it meant Stephanie would have been dead. But truth was truth.

Ivy wanted Carter in their family more than anything.

She put her phone on speaker. "Jennifer, Walker is here. The children are in the next room, though, so please speak softly."

"This good?" When Ivy said yes, Jennifer continued, "Stephanie was found in her apartment. She had a heart attack early Sunday morning but survived. She's in the hospital now and wants to know if you can keep Carter."

Ivy swallowed hard. Disappointment and yet—she'd take what she could for Carter's sake and his sisters'. "Of course. How long do we expect she'll need?"

Walker squeezed her fingers, his eyes haunted with the same sadness.

"No, you don't understand," Jennifer said even softer. "Stephanie has terminated her family rights. Her son had already given his up to her, and she says even once she recovers, she's not capable of raising Carter anymore. As parents to his siblings, you are now the first in line for priority if you want to adopt—"

"Yes." Walker and Ivy said it at the exact same moment.

Out of nowhere, laughter started deep in Ivy's heart. "Yes, we definitely want him," she assured Jennifer.

"Agreed," Walker said clearly. "What do we need to do?"

"Wait an hour for me to get to your house? I'm at the hospital. Stephanie has already signed the paperwork. I need to come and get signatures from you, and he'll be yours."

Ivy couldn't speak. Could barely breathe. It didn't seem possible.

Walker's strong arms came around her as he took the phone

from her trembling fingers. "Jennifer, thank you. You can't imagine how happy we are right now."

"You're welcome. I think someone else is going to be very happy too. Well, three someones, but especially Carter. Do you want to wait until I'm there to tell him or go ahead now? Because as far as I'm concerned, you're good to go."

Ivy glanced toward the living room. The girls were still quietly reading, and Carter was fast asleep, now covered with Harper's new favorite blanket.

Walker had seen the same thing. "He's sleeping. We'll play it by ear. See you soon."

He laid the phone on the counter and pulled Ivy into his arms.

Her body quivered with uncontrolled emotion. Brilliant joy, lingering fear. "He's really ours?"

"He really is." Walker's voice broke slightly.

Ivy eased them apart far enough to cup his face in her hands. "I'm sorry for speaking without us talking about it."

He grinned. "Notice I did the same? But Snow, we *had* talked about it. Many times. We've both said we wished we could make Carter's life better, and now we can."

Ivy leaned her head on Walker's chest and stared across the room at the children in the living room. *Their* children, hers and Walker's. Theirs to raise and care for.

Theirs to love.

Walker whispered softly, "Let's let him sleep for a bit longer, but I think we should talk to him before Jennifer gets here. He was worried about being taken away to a new foster home. Let's nip that concern in the bud."

"Agreed." But Ivy stayed there for another sweet moment, drawing strength from Walker, offering her love and support back.

Harper began to fidget, discarding her book and climbing

up on Ivy's chair to bounce on the cushion. She sang quietly, a counting song about horses, dogs, and chickens.

Chloe slipped onto the couch beside Carter. He stirred then sat up abruptly when he spotted his sister. His head spun to the side, and relief shone in his eyes when he spotted Ivy and Walker approaching. Followed quickly by worry.

"You must still be tired," Ivy offered gently as she sat on the couch beside him.

Carter shrugged.

Walker settled on the coffee table across from them. His steady gaze fixed on Carter. "We have some important things to tell you, and Chloe, and Harper. But first, your grandma's not dead. She's very sick, but she's going to get better. Okay?"

A choked cry escaped Carter. "She wouldn't wake up," he insisted.

"Because she was sick, but she's getting taken care of now," Walker repeated. His gaze darted to Ivy's. "But she will need to rest more in the future and be very careful to stay healthy. So she's asked us, Ivy and I, to take care of you."

Carter's eyes widened. He clutched Chloe's hand in a death grip. "You'll be my foster parents?"

Ivy scooped his free hand into hers. Walker wrapped his fingers around them both, holding tight, protecting. Offering strength as always.

"This isn't temporary," Ivy said softly. "We'll be your forever parents, just like with Chloe and Harper. You'll be our son."

She'd expected a reaction—tears maybe. More confusion.

What they got was two children in motion.

Carter threw himself at Ivy, clutching her tightly as he cried against her neck. Chloe all but leapt at Walker. She wept openly, her sobs bringing Harper over to see what the matter was.

Harper eyed both her bawling siblings, and for a second, her lower lip quivered as if she might sympathy cry.

Instead, she took a deep breath then patted Chloe's back. "See? Daddy's a good helper."

She turned to Carter and offered the same soothing physical contact, easing in close to speak to Ivy. "Mommy hugs make things better."

Ivy fought for control. She got caught up in the joy she felt inside and let it flow into her words. "I'm glad. Are you happy, Harper?"

The little girl nodded then eyed the kitchen. "I'm hungry. Can I have a snack?"

Ivy laughed. "Yes. Let's go make a snack together, all of us. Jennifer will be here soon. She has the permission papers so Carter can join our family. We should make an extra snack for her."

Because while the children liked Jennifer, Ivy didn't want the social worker's arrival to make Carter think he could be taken away.

Ivy squeezed Carter again, wondering at the sensation of the sturdy boy cradled in her lap. She lifted his chin. "Want to come help Mommy and Harper make snacks?"

He wiped at his eyes then nodded.

By the time Jennifer got there, snacks were on the table, juice glasses were poured, and an impromptu celebration was ready to begin.

Jennifer stepped into the house the instant Walker answered the buzzer, glancing over the children assembled at the table. "Hi, Carter. Rough day, hey, buddy?"

He nodded.

She paced over to Ivy and offered a hug. "Just a little more," she promised before settling in the chair next to Carter. "You heard that your grandma is going to be okay, yes?"

Carter sniffled then nodded again.

"Scary, huh?"

"Yeah." He stared at the papers Jennifer pulled from her shoulder bag. "They said I get to stay here."

"Ivy and Walker have already done everything they need to have permission to be your parents. The next thing I need for them to do is sign a couple of these pages." She ruffled his hair for a second. "I'm pretty sure I know the answer to this, but I'm supposed to ask. Do you want to stay here with Chloe and Harper? Are you okay with Mr. and Mrs. Stone becoming your parents—"

"Yes." Carter got the word out before she'd even finished the question. He nodded like a little bird at a feeder. "I like them. And Chloe and Harper. I want to be with my sisters."

Jennifer folded her hands, a pleased expression rising. "Well, then, let me steal them away for a moment."

She rose and crossed quickly to the island counter. A moment later she'd spread out some papers and offered Ivy a pen. "The same as you signed for Chloe and Harper. Transfer of family rights and full adoption. We'll have to file them with the courts, so you won't get the official papers for maybe six months, but there's no one family-wise who can contest your right to him. You put in the time waiting already. There's no reason to make any of you wait any longer."

The papers were familiar, and Ivy hurried to add her name.

Walker followed then gathered Ivy against his side. "Is that it?"

"That's it," Jennifer said brightly, smiling at Carter. "You are officially a member of the Stone family."

He blinked, dipped his chin, and stared at the table. Even from a few steps away, Ivy could see his flushed cheeks and the tears slipping free. Chloe wrapped her arms around him and hugged him fiercely.

"We made you a snack," Harper informed Jennifer, tugging at her sleeve and holding out a colourful bag filled with cereal. "We're ce'brating."

"I bet you are," Jennifer said kindly as she accepted the gift. "Let me take that for the road if you don't mind. I need to get home to my little girl."

"Thank you for doing all this so quickly," Walker said, moving to guide her to the door.

"Of course." Jennifer slipped her feet into her shoes and pulled the door open. "I'll be in touch this week with all the final documents I have right now. Plus, I'll contact Stephanie and see when you can pick up Carter's things."

"Check if she's up for visitors, please?" Ivy glanced at Carter. "I know he'd like to see for himself that she's okay."

Jennifer nodded. "Will do. In the meantime, congratulations. And thank you. I'm glad Carter's got you."

When Jennifer was gone, the house seemed strangely quiet. Ivy leaned her head against Walker's chest, his arm around her holding tight.

As she stared at their family—now five.

Joy wasn't a big enough word for what she felt inside.

EPILOGUE

Six weeks later

Blood poured from Carter's nose, but his expression said he was proud instead of frightened. "Everything was going great until that branch broke," he shared enthusiastically.

Walker fought to keep from grinning then figured *what the hell.* "You're lucky you didn't break your arm," he informed his son, pressing his handkerchief to Carter's nose and squeezing to stem the flow. "You're lucky your sisters didn't follow you."

Carter shrugged. "Chloe says climbing trees is for squirrels. And Harper did it last week already."

God Almighty. "Of course she did."

The three children were thick as thieves, but each of them was turning out to be as different as they came. Walker couldn't get over it and kind of didn't want to. Each day discovering who they were, and where they were going, amazed him.

Although he feared Harper's daredevil habits would make

him grey before his brothers. So far, Walker had discovered her walking the ridgeline of the horse stable, tightrope walking the railing of the arena, and climbing out her and Chloe's bedroom window to rescue a spider.

Ivy had simply smiled and said, "You'd think she had your genes, Dynamite."

Sweet memories were already gathering.

Carter's grandmother was still fragile, but they'd taken Carter and the girls to visit her. Stephanie still didn't seem immensely interested in time with her grandson, but she had seemed touched that Walker and Ivy had thought to come.

Who knew what might happen in the future? But for now, staying in contact was the right thing to do.

Carter leaned against Walker, wiggling his nose as he brushed the dirt from his arms. "Do we still get to go to Grandma Sophie and Grandpa's for supper?"

"Think you're up to it?" Walker asked, just to see what the kid would say.

They'd been an official family of five for just over a month. Walker's entire family, and Ivy's, had been over the moon when they'd announced Carter had also joined the clan.

The boy had returned the love wholeheartedly, especially when it came to having other guys around. Ivy's father was a huge hit, as were Walker's brothers, especially Dustin.

Now Carter nodded vigorously, pushing aside the handkerchief then checking his nostril with his fingers. "It stopped. I really want to see them. And Auntie Rose's boyfriend. He's supposed to have a cool accent."

"So I hear." Rose's date from the annual bachelor auction had caught the entire family's attention. He seemed far more serious than her previous boyfriends. Thus the family dinner invite.

Walker checked his son over, admiring the layer of dust and dirt. He could have sworn the kid had been clean half an hour ago. "Go take a bath. Then check with your mom. She might have some chores for you before we go."

"Okay." Carter was off running.

Walker slid carefully into the house, ready to rinse out the blood before anyone else noticed it.

No chance of that. Ivy stood at the island, supervising as Chloe carefully transferred cookies onto a sheet to be baked.

Ivy instantly spotted the messy evidence. "Limbs still mostly attached?" she asked.

"His nose is a little dented, but he's okay," Walker assured her before directing his attention to his middle child. "Yum. Something smells good. Do I get one?"

"Mommy and I are making Grandma's favourite cookies." Chloe put down the spatula and picked up one of the sugar cookies cooling on the tray. She stepped closer and offered it. "This one's for you, Daddy."

He didn't think the thrill of hearing that title would ever go away. Not for him, not for Ivy. "Special for *me*?"

She nodded and peeked at Ivy, then when she saw her mom was placing the tray in the oven, Chloe cupped her hand to her mouth and whispered, "I made it extra big."

"Just the way I like them. Thanks, kitten." He winked at her.

Ivy was watching, her smile soft, pleasure clear. "Want to grab a shower before we head over to my parents' house? There's time."

"Good idea." After his outdoor chores? Definitely.

He paused en route to see what their youngest was up to.

He found Harper in the reading room that faced the outdoors, her back to the hallway. She'd placed toys in rows on the couch and footstool—stuffed animals, dolls, spacemen.

"This is your family. See?" Harper lifted her well-worn moose in the air and had him greet the others one by one. "This is Gamma, and Gampa. Auntie Tansy and Auntie Rose and Auntie Fern. Uncle Caleb and Auntie 'mara."

She went through every one of the family and didn't miss a single person.

Walker watched until the very end then slipped away unseen, wonder filling him.

There was a moment before they all headed out the door to dinner. Ivy had just finished helping Harper put her coat on. Their youngest was singing as usual. Carter was rolling on the floor, making what Walker assumed were bull noises. Chloe held the bag of freshly baked cookies with pride in her eyes and a smile on her lips as she watched her brother.

Walker held Ivy's coat for her. "Did you imagine it would be like this?" he asked softly.

She slid an arm around him and hugged him tight, her gaze dancing over their family. "It's so much more than I ever dreamed," she admitted. "And the best part of it all is that I get to enjoy every minute with you." Her eyes sparkled. "I love you."

"Love you too." He grinned and accepted her kiss willingly, children milling around their legs. The chaos and love of the moment was bright and rich.

As he broke the kiss, Ivy whispered the only words that still needed to be said. "Although, I think we might need a dog."

Walker threw back his head and laughed.

Family, forever.

ABOUT THE AUTHOR

New York Times and *USA Today* bestselling author Vivian Arend loves to share the products of her over-active imagination with her readers. She writes contemporary, western, and light-hearted paranormal romances. The stories are humorous yet emotional, usually with a large cast of family or friends, and a guaranteed happily-ever-after. Vivian lives in British Columbia, Canada, with her husband of many years—her inspiration for every hero and a willing companion for all sorts of adventures.

www.vivianarend.com

www.ingramcontent.com/pod-product-compliance
Lightning Source LLC
Chambersburg PA
CBHW051231210726
48290CB00003B/897